All in Good Time

All in Good Time

By EDWARD ORMONDROYD

Drawings by Ruth Robbins

PARNASSUS PRESS BERKELEY, CALIFORNIA

COPYRIGHT © 1975 BY EDWARD ORMONDROYD FOR STORY
COPYRIGHT © 1975 BY RUTH ROBBINS FOR DRAWINGS
LIBRARY OF CONGRESS CATALOG CARD NUMBER 75–1688
PUBLISHED BY PARNASSUS PRESS
PRINTED IN THE UNITED STATES OF AMERICA
ISBN 0–87466 TR–072–6 LIB–073–4

For Joan,
and the anonymous toucans who started it all.

⇥⇥⇥⇥ ⇤⇤⇤⇤

◄§ 1. SUSAN SHAW AGAIN ▷

One Friday in August, late in the morning, Susan Shaw came into my life again, more than a year and a half after she had vanished from Ward Street and the twentieth century.

It had been a phone call that told me of her disappearance, and it was another that served to bring our paths so curiously together again. But this time I had no inkling that she would be involved; her name wasn't mentioned, and what I heard on the phone was mostly noise. It was the kind of call you can't take seriously. If I hadn't been in trouble with my work, nothing would have come of it. But I was in trouble. I had been trying to write for two hours, without any success whatsoever. When that idiot phone began to ring, my first impulse was to tear it off the wall and throw it out the window into Ward Street; and when I finally answered, it was in a very surly fashion.

There was a moment of silence at the other end, followed by a thin, tremulous gasp, as though someone very far away were trying to catch a breath. And then I jumped. Out of the receiver came a *BL-L-LA-A-AAATT BL-L-LAAAAMMBRMRMRM* that nearly ruptured my

7

eardrum. It sounded like some fool revving up an engine without a muffler. I was just about to slam the phone down when a little quavery feminine voice began to talk through the racket. I heard the word "books."

"What?" I yelled.

"Books," the voice doddered. "A box of—"

BLAHAHAHAAAAMMM!

"Can't *hear* you!"

"At the" *brmmm*-rm-rm "Historical Association" *vrooooooOOOM!* "very important" *blat-blat*-blammm.

"Are you sure you've got the right number?"

She mentioned a number. It came through a lot of *rrrrrr* and *fap fap fap*, but it was mine.

"Who is this, please?" I asked.

She gave a wavery little gasp, and then there was such an insane crescendo from that motor that I had to jerk the phone away from my ear; and when I was ready to listen again, there was only the sound of the dial tone.

Some kind of dumb practical joke . . .

I went back to my desk. It was hot outside; a heat wave had been predicted. It was even hotter inside. For half an hour I waited for the next word to come, and then stood up again with a sigh. It was going to be one of those days . . . Well, sometimes when my head is stuck I can get it moving again by taking a walk. And now that the place had been mentioned, why not drop in on the Historical Association? It was the right distance, and I hadn't seen Charles for a while. He is Vice-President of the Association, and a good friend of mine.

I headed for the elevator—the same elevator in which Susan and her father had disappeared. But I didn't give them a thought as the old machine groaned its way with me down to the first floor. Why should I? That affair was over and done with.

8

⟨ ⟨ ⟨ ⟩ ⟩ ⟩

The headquarters of the Historical Association is a solemn old brownstone house. The hush of the past falls over everything as you step inside. Even the air has a kind of antique taste to it—much more breathable than the yellow-tinted stuff out in the streets.

"Edward! Good to see you again. Did you drop in for another look at your favorite mysterious picture?"

"Hello, Charles. No, not really—just out for a walk to clear my head. But now that you've mentioned it, I think I will."

And while he regarded me with an ironic air, I went over to the reading room wall where an old dark brown photograph was displayed. It showed a Victorian family group standing in front of a tall, narrow, much-decorated house. The group, from left to right, consisted of a boy in uniform, a lovely woman holding a baby, a man with a mustache, and two girls. The girl on the far right had a satisfied little smile on her face; and as always, I found myself smiling back at her.

"By the way, Charles," I said, turning back to him, "there wouldn't happen to be some books here for me, would there?"

"No, not that I know of. Why?"

"Oh, somebody called me up, and imitated a little old lady in the middle of a motorcycle race, and said there was a box of books here."

"Oh? I'm the only one here who knows you—and I don't do imitations."

"Well, it must have been somebody trying to be funny, then."

"People do dump books on us, though—old junk from

9

attics and so forth. Want to see if any have come in recently?"

"Oh . . ." I began to shrug, but he had already turned away; so I followed until we came to a room in the back of the building, where boxes and manuscripts and pictures and bundles of letters and antique household articles and weapons were stacked all over.

"Well!" he said. "How's that for a coincidence?"

On the floor stood a breakfast-food carton heaped with dingy volumes. We picked them out, one by one: sixty-year-old novels, a book of verse entitled *Heart Throbs,* Stodgeley's *Lectures,* little green Latin textbooks . . . At the bottom of the heap a battered blue leather volume caught my notice. There was no title on the spine, none on the front cover. I opened it: lined pages; handwriting —a fast loopy scrawl. Some kind of journal or diary . . . On the first page—

"Hey!" Charles cried. "Are you all right?" He swept a pile of letters from a chair and pushed it toward me. I sat, or rather fell, on it. He hovered over me, saying, "Glass of water?"

"No," I gasped. "It's all right—just a shock. Oh, good lord! Oh, my word! Charles, I—I want this book."

He took it from my shaking hands and riffled through it. "Hmm—an original document. Well, I don't know, Edward, I don't know. Mmm . . ." A little curl appeared at the corners of his mouth. "I might consider it."

I reached for the book, but he put it behind his back. "Not just yet," he said. "I'm going to blackmail you a little. You want this book. *I* want an explanation. Ever since I first showed you that old photograph out there you've been acting like the cat that swallowed the cream. You know something about that picture that I don't and I want to know what it is."

"Charles, I told you I was going to write a book about all that, and I did. It's coming out next month, as a matter of fact. You can read—"

"I don't want to wait another month. I've already waited more than a year."

"Well . . . you're not going to believe any of it."

"I want to hear it anyway."

"Oh, all right," I sighed. "Brace yourself."

⊰⊰⊰⊱⊱⊱

"Let's see, now . . . I guess I'd better identify everybody first. The name of the family in the photograph is Shaw. The woman with the baby was a widow when she married Mr. Shaw—her name before that was Walker. The boy in the uniform and the tall, dreamy-looking girl are her children, Robert and Victoria. The girl on the right with the little smile is Susan. She's Mr. Shaw's daughter. Got it all straight?

"It looks like a typical nineteenth-century family, doesn't it? Well, it is—and it isn't. The fact of the matter is that Mr. Shaw and Susan come—came—from the twentieth century. They were living in my apartment building on Ward Street not two years ago. Don't make those faces, Charles; you asked for this. Mr. Shaw was an accountant for a firm in the city, and Susan went to school somewhere in this part of town.

"One day in March last year she was coming home from school when she met a strange old lady in the street. The old lady asked for help, and Susan gave it to her, and the old lady thanked her by saying, 'I'll give you three.' She was a witch, you see. Don't look like that, Charles. It turned out that she meant three rides on the elevator in our apartment building—rides into the past.

Susan took the first one when she got home, although all she intended to do was go up to the seventh floor, the top, to look at the view. What happened was that the elevator kept on going *past* the seventh floor; and when it stopped, and she got out, she was in a hallway of that house in the photograph, and it was early summer of the year 1881.

"She landed in an interesting situation. A beautiful widow named Mrs. Walker was living in the house. She had a daughter, Victoria, who was about Susan's age, and a son, Robert, who was younger. There was also a servant named Maggie, and a cat named Toby. Mrs. Walker was being courted by a man named Sweeney. She wasn't in love with him, but she was on the point of accepting him because her money was almost gone, and she wanted to secure a future for her children. Victoria was sure that Mr. Sweeney was a scoundrel who was only interested in her mother because he thought she was rich. So Victoria had gone to a wishing well and dropped her locket in and wished for someone to come and chase Mr. Sweeney away. That's apparently why the witch had sent Susan there.

"And she did chase Mr. Sweeney away, too. She and Victoria and Robert made up a story that Mrs. Walker had been robbed of all her money by a swindler, and had just caught the smallpox as well. Susan pretended to be a servant girl who was running away from all this disaster. She met Mr. Sweeney in the back yard of the house next door, where he was boarding with some people named Hollister. She was an excellent actress, and convinced Mr. Sweeney that the story was true. He took to his heels at once, proving that Victoria's suspicions had been correct.

"Well, the children didn't know it, but Mrs. Walker

really had lost all her money. She told them—Robert and Victoria, that is—she never did learn about Susan until much later—she told them what the situation was, and started making plans to sell the house, and wrote to her Cousin Jane for advice and help.

"But Susan thought she could save the situation because she knew where a treasure was buried. Just before she'd come up the elevator she had been reading the newspaper. There had been a front-page story about a bulldozer operator who had uncovered thousands of dollars in pre-Civil War gold coins at a construction site not far from the apartment house. There was a map with the story. Susan's idea was that she would go down the elevator to the twentieth century—she had three rides through time, remember—get the newspaper with the map, take it back to 1881, and then she and Victoria and Robert could find the treasure themselves. And that's what happened. It was all open country back then, you see, and by following the map and pacing off what would someday be city blocks, they found the place and dug up the treasure. It was a lot harder than I'm making it sound, of course."

"Hold it—hold it!" Charles interrupted. "If they dug up the treasure in 1881, how could a bulldozer operator dig it up again last year?"

"Well, as it turned out, he didn't. He couldn't. After the children found the treasure, they happened to look at the newspaper—and there was no longer any such story on the front page. It hadn't happened after all, because now it couldn't. The kids called it 'changing history.' "

"I don't get it."

"It's what's known as a time paradox, Charles. All it means is that if you can travel in time, you can, oh, sort of erase things that *have* happened where you came from so that they *won't* have happened when you go back. For all I know, you might even be able to do something in the present that could change the past.

"Anyway, they had the treasure, and they were bringing it back that night to hide it in the stable when Susan sprained her ankle. They couldn't carry her and all that heavy gold too, so they hid the treasure under a bramble bush by the roadside, and Susan spent the night in the stable. Next morning she had an idea. She loved Victoria and Robert, and she thought Mrs. Walker was marvelous. Her own mother had been dead several years. Why couldn't she go back to the twentieth century and bring her father up the elevator? She and Victoria thought that if Mr. Shaw and Mrs. Walker met, they would fall in love and get married, and then they could all live happily together in the nineteenth century. If they *didn't* fall in love, then Susan and her father would come back to the twentieth century. At least the Walkers would be saved from their predicament, because the treasure would stay with them.

"She thought it was worth trying, anyhow. So she came down the elevator, and found that she had created quite a mystery by her absence. She'd been gone from the apartment building for several days, you know, and everyone thought she'd been kidnapped. There was a detective working on the case, and her father was half crazy with worry. So there was quite a hullaballoo when she suddenly appeared again wearing nineteenth-century clothes. When she was finally alone with her father she told him the whole story. There was a snoopy cleaning woman, Mrs. Clutchett, who had been in on the mystery from the beginning, and she listened to Susan through the keyhole and told me—that's how I know about it. (Mrs. Clutchett married a flying saucer crank

14

last year and moved across town, but I can put you in touch with her, Charles, if you want to hear all this from another source.)

"Nobody believed Susan's story, including me at first. Her father thought she had had some sort of mental breakdown, and he was determined to get her to a psychiatrist. She made a bargain with him; she'd go to the psychiatrist if he would first go up the elevator with her to see for himself whether or not her story was true. She didn't hide anything from him, either. She told him frankly that she intended to arrange a meeting with Mrs. Walker, and that she hoped they would fall in love and get married. He agreed to go because he was afraid her madness might become worse if he refused. She even talked him into wearing a nineteenth-century costume for the occasion. They went up on a Saturday night. Our janitor, Mr. Bodoni, saw them getting on the elevator. He thought by the way they were dressed that they were going to a costume party. He was the last person ever to see them. They vanished without a trace. That's a fact, Charles. Whatever you think of the rest of the story, Susan and her father did disappear. I've got newspaper clippings to prove it."

"All right, I'll take your word for that part of it. But the rest—!"

"I know it sounds crazy. But after I did a little checking up, I decided that I believed it, anyway—maybe because my taste runs to that sort of thing. The clincher was when you asked me over to see the new Historical Association headquarters, and I saw that old photograph on the wall. I knew it was true then. I mean, there they all are! It's obvious that everything turned out the way Susan hoped it would."

"Are you absolutely sure that those are the people you

think they are?"

"Well, I'm sure about Susan."

"Mmm . . ."

"You're an awful skeptic, Charles. Well, nuts to you. I've given you the explanation you asked for. Now may I have that book?"

He made no move to hand it over. "You know, I thought you were going to pass out when you looked into this book. Now tell me what *that* was about, and it's yours."

"Oh, all right. I'm finding it a little hard to believe this part of it myself . . . Well, when Mr. Bodoni saw the Shaws getting on the elevator he noticed that they were both carrying something. Mr. Shaw was carrying a black cat—Toby, the Walkers' cat, who'd come to the twentieth century by mistake with Susan. And Susan was carrying—brace yourself again, Charles—Susan was carrying a diary. A blue leather book. The book you're holding right now."

"Oh, come on!"

"I know, I know! But just read the first sentence, will you?"

He read aloud, " 'Daddy and I went up the elevator last night.' " His voice trailed off on the word "night," and he let out a long whistle.

"See what I mean? Now may I have it?"

"Incredible . . ." he murmured. "Yes, you may have it. Just one more favor, though? Will you read it here so I can read along with you?"

Daddy and I went up the elevator last night.
Poor Daddy—he was in a state. We'd had
a terrible day. Everybody kept interrupting,
and he tried to get an appointment for me
without any luck, and he was embarrassed
by his costume, and when we finally got
there . . .

"Hallucinations," Mr. Shaw said into the telephone. "She thinks she's gone into the past, and she says she wants to go back again and take me with her.—No. First time anything like this has happened.—No, no depression.—No, her health has been fine.—No, she's acting normally otherwise.—Well, she looks—she looks happy."

"I am happy," Susan said.

"Thursday!" Mr. Shaw went on. "No, I'm sorry, it really has to be sooner than that.—Oh." He banged down the receiver, wiped his hand over his face, and burst out, "What's the matter with these quacks, anyway? Just because I can't tell 'em that you're rigid as a board and foaming at the mouth, they won't take me seriously. 'Nothing to be alarmed about,' he says, 'I can see you Thursday.' "

"I can wait till Thursday, Daddy."

"We're seeing somebody today, or Monday afternoon at the latest. Let's see, who's next?" He ran his finger down a column in the telephone directory.

She wanted to say, "We won't be here Monday," but she refrained. He was doing what he felt he had to do, and once an appointment was made he would feel better.

17

The main thing was that he had agreed to go up the elevator with her to meet Mrs. Walker. She had agreed, as her side of the bargain, to see a psychiatrist. Maybe it was unfair of her to make such a promise, knowing that she would never have to keep it.

Oh, dear, he was slamming down the receiver again . . .

"Daddy, why don't we have some lunch now, and then you can try again when you're a little more calm?"

But he was already dialling the next number. 'Please,' she prayed, 'let it be somebody who isn't busy.' She *had* to get her father calmed down soon, because there was still the matter of his costume to take care of. She was all set with the dress and shoes Victoria had lent her, but he had nothing. It was unthinkable that they introduce him to Mrs. Walker in his twentieth-century business suit, or the grey chinos that he had on now. He had agreed under duress to wear a costume, but she knew it was going to be difficult to get him right down to it; and they had to go out and buy one before the stores closed.

The doorbell rang. ". . . hallucinations," Mr. Shaw was saying into the telephone for the twentieth time. He motioned toward the door with his eyes. She didn't want to open it. The bell rang again before her reluctant hand turned the knob.

It was the man who had started to pester her with questions that morning the minute she had stepped out of the elevator.

"Hello, Susan," he said. "How are you feeling now?"

"Oh . . . all right," she answered, not stepping aside to let him in.

He pushed in anyway. "Susan," he said, "let's sit down and have a little heart-to-heart talk, shall we? My name is Mr. Haugen. I'm a detective."

Oh, good grief . . . "I'm all right," she said. "Nothing happened to me. Really."

Her father put down the receiver and said, "Another quack trying to tell me everything can wait. Hello, Mr. Haugen."

"Hello, Mr. Shaw. Susan and I were just going to get it all straightened out, now that she's feeling better."

The doorbell rang. It was the couple from next door, the ones who always turned on their television set full blast the first thing in the morning. Ugh! Their tongues were practically hanging down to their waistlines with curiosity. Oh yes, she was fine, everything was all right, she'd just been staying with friends, there'd been a little mix-up, pardon me, busy right now. She shut the door on their gleaming eyes.

"You can be perfectly frank with me, Susan," Detective Haugen said. He wasn't going to believe the truth any more than her father did . . . It was time to put on an act. She made her chin tremble, and said in a wavering voice, "Can I talk about it—later?"

"She's still kind of distraught," her father said.

The doorbell rang. Mr. Shaw grabbed his hair and pulled it. "I'll drop by later," Detective Haugen said, easing himself out the door. "Oop! Pardon me, ma'am."

Mrs. Clutchett came down on them like a tornado.

"Merciful heavens, what're *you* doing up, child? You ought to be in bed with a nice hot cup of cocoa. And limping—still limping! D'you mean to say she hasn't been taken to a doctor *yet*, Mr. Shaw? Why, goodness, don't try to tell *me* it isn't anything, missy! Believe you me, you neglect something like that and the first thing you know complications can set in! And you, sir, standing around like a bump on a log or I don't-know-what while this poor motherless child wastes away from neglect and misunderstanding!" She emphasized the word "motherless" with a little shake of her head. "Well, Mr. Shaw, I don't care if heaven itself falls, I *will* speak my mind concerning a subject of which you know very well what I'm speaking about. Not that I don't respect your feelings, but things have come to the point of no return, as they say, so *if* you will be so kind as to give me a few minutes of your valuable time—alone."

He threw one agonized look over his shoulder at Susan before Mrs. Clutchett swept him into the kitchen and shut the door.

'Trying to talk him into marrying someone again,' Susan thought. 'Poor Daddy . . . and I'm doing the same thing. But I won't have to do any talking, he'll just look at Mrs. Walker and she'll look at him—and pow! Good grief, look at the time! I'm going to have to get his costume myself, or we'll never make it . . . Oh, and a diary! Vicky's diary was so much fun . . .'

She scribbled a note: "Dear Daddy, I haven't disappeared again, I just have to buy some things. I'll be right back," and dashed out of the apartment.

⊰ ⊰ ⊰ ⊱ ⊱ ⊱

"I feel like an idiot in this get-up."

"It's late, Daddy, nobody's going to see us. Here, hold Toby, will you please? I can't handle him and my diary both." She peered out the door. "All clear! Come on!"

They hurried across the hallway. Susan pressed the button, and somewhere below the elevator groaned into action.

"Oh, good night!" Mr. Shaw muttered. "Why did he have to pick *now*?"

Mr. Bodoni was ambling down the hallway, chewing

20

his cigar and carrying a bundle of newspapers under his arm. He stopped when he saw them, and began to grin.

Susan didn't care. Her project was launched now, and joy was bubbling inside her so strongly that she felt as though she could soar like a balloon.

"Fancy dress party, hah?" Mr. Bodoni said. "Costoom party?"

She smiled at him, loving him. There, he'd given them the perfect excuse for looking as they did. Her father didn't have to feel embarrassed now. Why should he mutter like that?

The door wheezed open and they got in. Oh, she was going to float, she'd have to hold on to something to keep her feet on the ground! "Goodbye, Mr. Bodoni!" she called, pressing the seventh-floor button.

"Yeah," he said. "Have a good time."

"Flaming moron!" Mr. Shaw muttered; and then the door closed, and they were on their way.

Toby, who had been growing tense ever since leaving the apartment, moaned as the elevator heaved itself into motion.

"OW!" Mr. Shaw roared.

"Oh, Daddy, I'm sorry! He's such a brute when he gets in here; I forgot. Let me take him."

Toby's claws had sunk deep and he would not turn loose. The three of them struggled for several floors, panting and *ow*ing and yowling.

"I've had it!" Mr. Shaw cried. "This—blasted—animal —gets—*out!*" He reached for the buttons.

"No!" she yelped, throwing herself against him. "We have to take him back! I promised Vicky."

"We can come back for him later when we—ouch! —have a box to put him in."

"Why can't you understand, Daddy? When we get

there, there's only half a trip left. If we come down again we'll never be able to get back." She had one of Toby's paws loose now. He said "Ow-w-w-w!" blowing his fishy breath on her.

"Hey!" Mr. Shaw said—but not to her. He was staring over her head. She glanced up. The arrow had come to rest on 7, but the elevator was still rising. There was a sensation of thickness in the air.

"It's all right!" she said. "That's the worst part, that sort of ooshy feeling when it goes through."

"There's something wrong with the mechanism. I'm going to speak to Bodoni about this—it could be dangerous."

The elevator stopped, and the door trundled open. There was a sound of tearing cloth as Toby twisted free, leaped to the floor, and vanished.

"Hey!" Mr. Shaw said again. "What's the matter with the—?"

"Sssh!"

Her hiss was so urgent that he lowered his voice. "The lights," he continued, *sotto voce*. "Look, they're practically out. They are out. This whole place goes to ruin while that idiot Bodoni fumbles around with his newspapers!"

"Sssh!" she whispered again. "We really have to be quiet, Daddy. Don't worry about the lights, there aren't any up here. I wonder where Vicky is—she was supposed to meet us. Well, she left us a candle anyway. Come on."

They stepped out into the hallway. Susan turned and pressed the first-floor button. The elevator door sighed and trundled shut, eclipsing the electric light within. They were left in the soft orange glow of candlelight.

"Say," Mr. Shaw murmured, "it really is different up

here now, isn't it? Wasn't like this a few days ago. Somebody's been doing a lot of fast work." He gazed about at the oak wainscotting, the dark velvet curtains, the grandfather clock, the little marble-topped table on which stood a stuffed owl under a glass bell and a bowl of paper flowers and a half-consumed candle. "Antiques!" he exclaimed. "They could get stolen, lying around like this."

"Daddy," she whispered, "come on, we really have to go. You can look at all this later." She took his sleeve in one hand, picked up the candlestick in the other, and began to pull him toward the back of the house. She was wondering if something had gone wrong. Victoria should have been waiting for them. Well, the best thing now was to get out to the stable and wait for Victoria there . . .

"Ssst!" she hissed, tightening her grip on his sleeve so suddenly that he jumped. She looked back over her shoulder. He turned to look too. There was nothing at that end of the hallway but dark shadows.

Somewhere in the front of the house there was a muffled sliding sound, and a heavy thump.

"Vicky?" Susan whispered.

Silence.

"Maybe it was Toby," she murmured. "Come on."

"Susie, I am very tired. I've been under a terrific strain since you disappeared Wednesday night. I think maybe I'm beginning to understand why you're having the kind of hallucinations you have—I mean, obviously there's something out of whack in the elevator, and that fool Bodoni has let all the lights up here burn out, and there's been some redecoration. All right. But the answer is, so what? We're still on the seventh floor. Now let's go down and go to bed."

"Daddy, will you please please just come outside for a minute before you make up your mind? Please?"

"What? My dear child, it's under forty degrees out there, and the wind's blowing!"

"Well, can't we just stick our noses out, then? I'll tell you what: if it is under forty degrees and the wind is blowing, I promise we'll go back right away."

"Oh . . . all right. Good night, you're a stubborn one! Where are we going, the fire escape?"

"No."

They had reached a door; she wasn't sure, but hoped it was the door to the kitchen. She opened it with care. A little draft burst through and extinguished the candle, but not before she had seen that it was the kitchen on the other side. They were all right, then. She pulled her father in and shut the door behind them.

"Susan!" he whispered, clutching her shoulder. "We shouldn't be sneaking into somebody's apartment like this!"

"It's all right, we're just going to zip through."

They zipped through. She opened the back door, and they stepped out on the porch.

The sweet summer smell of damp earth and grass enveloped them. Frogs were shouting "Brrreep brrreep!" in the pond nearby. The sky glittered with stars and moonlight from horizon to zenith. The shrubbery-dotted back yard, the stable, the surrounding fields and woods, were drawn in charcoal and silver.

"O-o-oh!" she sighed, taking a deep breath.

Mr. Shaw made a shuddery noise and staggered against her. "I want to sit down," he said in a choked voice. She helped him down. "Where are we?" he whispered.

"Oh, Daddy!" she sighed. "I've told you and *told* you."

24

She sat down beside him and squeezed his trembling hand. "You're going to love it in a minute. You'll see."

⊰ 3. A CLOUD ON THE HORIZON ⊱

> *. . . in the stable. Daddy didn't say anything for so long that I began to worry. Then Vicky and Bobbie came out. They hadn't been able to meet us because Maggie had been prowling around. Daddy made a hit with Bobbie, and Vicky approves of him too. They had some bad news, though. We'll have to work fast . . .*

"Sue?"

Straw rustled as Susan and Mr. Shaw gave a start in the darkness.

"Is that you, Vicky?"

"Yes! And Bobbie." Two forms appeared in silhouette against the stars in the doorway, and vanished again as Robert and Victoria came into the inky shadows of the stable. "Thank goodness!" Victoria's voice went on. "It *was* you, then! We couldn't tell whether you or Maggie had taken the candle, so we had to come out and see."

"Maggie?" Susan said.

"Yes. Oh, the suspense was dreadful! You see, we left a lighted candle for you on the hallway table, in case you arrived before it was safe for us to come down. We waited and waited, and finally we crept downstairs, and heavens!—there was Maggie in her nightgown, standing in the parlor!"

"I think she was trying to catch me," Robert said. "There's a new cake in the pantry, and she knows I'd like to forage a little of it."

"Anyway, we had to retreat upstairs again and wait for*ever* until Maggie went back to bed, and when we came down the candle was gone; and we didn't know if you'd come or if she'd taken it."

"It was us," Susan said. "Thank you for the candle. Come here, Daddy, I want you to meet the—oh, how am I going to introduce you all in the dark?"

"A soldier is always prepared," Robert announced. There was a click, and a beam of light pierced the darkness. He had opened the shutter of his bull's-eye lantern.

"Victoria Walker, Robert Walker," Susan said, suddenly feeling awkward and shy. "Mr. Shaw, my father." Her heart began to pound. It was so important that they like each other . . . !

"Pleased to meet you, sir," Robert said, putting out his hand.

"My pleasure," Mr. Shaw said, shaking it.

"Charmed to make your acquaintance, Mr. Shaw," Victoria said. "Did you not find today's heat somewhat fatiguing?"

Mr. Shaw was not prepared for her Deportment Class voice. He mumbled, "Well, ah, yes, I mean no, actually," and then something got caught in his throat and he doubled over trying to *harumph* it clear again.

"Oh dear me!" Victoria cried. "I do hope you are not indisposed, sir?"

Mr. Shaw rallied. "No, no, thank you, frog in my throat, I'm all right. Really pleased to meet you, too.

26

I'm ah—it's just that—oh, look here, I'm having a hard time taking all this in. I mean, Susan's told me an incredible story about herself and you—"

"Oh, it's all true, sir," Robert said.

"Well, it's hard for me to—look, is it really the—? I mean, what year *is* it, actually?"

"1881, sir."

"Ah," Mr. Shaw said faintly. "I see . . . Who's President?"

"Mr. Garfield, sir."

"Mmm . . . 1881 . . . I can't seem to get my bearings. Is the, ah, Franco-Prussian war on? Or hasn't it begun?"

"Oh, no, sir, it's been over for some time now—ten years, as a matter of fact. There's no fighting going on anywhere now, I regret to say, except maybe the Transvaal."

"You *regret* to say!"

"Well, you see, sir, I have a professional interest. I want to be an officer in the Army when I grow up."

"Oh. Well, I guess these things seem different when you're young . . . I was an officer in the Army myself, and it was the happiest day in my life when I got my discharge."

"You were an officer, sir?" Robert said eagerly. "May I ask what rank?"

"First Lieutenant."

Robert's owlish eyes grew even rounder. "Did you see any action?"

"A little. Enough to last me a lifetime."

"Oh, come on, Bobbie," Susan interrupted, "you can talk about all that later. We have our own campaign to think about now. I mean," she checked herself, "*if* it's all right with both of you to—go ahead . . ."

"Oh, yes!" Robert said. "I should say so!"

"I am sure," Victoria said in her Deportment Class voice, "that there can be no impropriety in arranging a meeting between our mother and Mr. Shaw."

She had been covertly studying Mr. Shaw all during his conversation with Robert. There was a hesitancy in her manner now that made Susan ask, "What's the matter, Vicky?"

Victoria clasped her hands and lowered her eyes. "I fear it is dreadfully presumptuous of me," she murmured.

"Oh, Vick, for heaven's sake! What is the matter?"

"Well, you see—it's—I'm afraid that—Mr. Shaw's clothes—" and she finished up in a rush, "are-not-quite-the-thing," blushing so furiously that it was noticeable even by the light of the bull's-eye.

The Shaws burst out laughing. "Just what I thought myself," Mr. Shaw said. And Susan threw her arms around Victoria and said, "Oh, Vicky, why did you think we'd care if you told us?"

"Well, I was afraid that you might have gone to a lot of trouble."

"Oh, no—I just went to a theatrical costumer and asked for something suitable for the 'eighties. I never thought about men's styles changing from year to year, but they do, don't they?"

"I think they gave you the wrong period altogether, Sue. I mean, those lapels and the cut of the shoulders and that cravat—goodness, no one wears clothes like that now. It looks as strange as if he were to wear twentieth-century things."

"All right, we'll have to get something fashionable, then. What do you suggest?"

"There's Bardwell's," Robert said.

"Oh . . ." Victoria made a little face. "But it will have to be something like that, I'm afraid. Bardwell's Haberdashers and Gents' Outfitters," she explained to Susan. "They have ready-made clothes, but their taste leaves much to be desired . . . Well! I'm sure you can find something wearable there. A light-colored suit would be right for this time of year."

"We concluded that you ought to go into town anyway," Robert said. "It would look more real if you came to Hollisters' from town. What we thought was, you could find Jim Perkins at the railroad station, and ask him to recommend a place to stay in the country—"

"You have come to the countryside to take the air," Victoria said. "You're travelling for your health. Do you think you could manage to look pale?"

"Oh, we're both perfectly healthy," Susan said. "Why can't we be coming to the country for a vacation? It's better to keep things simple, you don't have to explain so much."

"I expect you're right," Victoria sighed. "It's just that a person recovering from a long illness is so—interesting. Particularly if the illness was connected with a broken heart."

"Oh, listen to that, will you?" Robert groaned.

"You have no more romance in your soul than a *toad*," his sister sniffed.

"Anyway, we ask Jim Perkins where to go—?"

"He's sure to recommend the Hollisters," Robert said. "I think they have a little agreement. He'll drive you out in his surrey for fifty cents—"

"And then when you're all settled in," Victoria went on, "you could happen to be walking about in the Hollisters' garden, Sue, and Bobbie and I could just happen to be out strolling ourselves, and we could happen to

29

meet each other, and our acquaintance could ripen into friendship with extraordinary rapidity—"

"Oh!" Robert said. "It had better be extraordinary rapidity! I just remembered—there isn't much time." He gave his sister a look.

She gasped, putting her hands to her mouth. "There's so much to think about, I quite forgot!"

"What is it?" Susan asked in alarm.

"It's Cousin Jane," Robert said glumly. "Oh, I wish Mama had never—"

"Now, Bobbie, you know Mama would never have written to Cousin Jane if the rest of the family weren't so far away. And she never asked Cousin Jane to come here—she only asked if we could go—"

"Well, it doesn't matter what she wrote or why. The thing is, Cousin Jane *is* coming here. Day after tomorrow, in the afternoon."

"But," Susan said, "didn't your Mama get the money and the note from her unknown admirer that we made up? I thought that was going to keep her from making hasty decisions."

"She'd already written," Victoria sighed. "And it wouldn't have made any difference anyway, as it turns out."

"What happened?"

"Why, we pretended that we'd found the money and the note on the doorstep," Victoria said. "She read the note several times and then she said, 'Well! Some eccentric and *anonymous* person wishes to make us the object of his charity,' and she put the money on the table. And I could tell by the way she did it that she would never touch it again . . . But you know, now that I think about it, I can't blame her. I mean, goodness, it might have been from some terrible person like Mr. Sweeney!

I'm afraid I was so carried away by the romantic aspect of the idea that I didn't think."

"So the upshot is," Robert went on, "that Cousin Jane . . ." His voice trailed off.

"But what's so terrible about Cousin Jane?" Susan asked.

Robert and Victoria looked at each other and sighed.

"She's—a Tartar," Victoria said.

"I'd rather face a regiment of Prussian cavalry than Cousin Jane," Robert said.

"But what can she *do*?"

"She can Disapprove," Victoria said.

"Do you think she's going to disapprove of Daddy?"

"I'm afraid so . . . In fact, I know she will."

The three of them turned their troubled faces toward Mr. Shaw. He was leaning with folded arms against a post.

"It's nothing to do with you, sir, personally," Robert explained. "She disapproves of men in general."

Mr. Shaw gave a little smile and said, "I see."

"Good grief!" Susan sighed. "It's beginning to sound so complicated . . . I'm sorry, Daddy, I thought everything would be simple and straightforward."

"Well, it is, as far as I can see," Mr. Shaw said. "You kids arrange a meeting, and we meet, and—" he lifted his shoulders "—there we are."

'Darn you, Daddy!' she thought. 'Can't you at least *act* as though you're looking forward to it?' "Yes!" she said, too loudly and too quickly, to cover up her embarrassment. "Have we forgotten anything?" she hurried on. "I guess not. Oh, wait, yes! Money! All I've got is an eagle. We'll need more for Daddy's clothes and something for the Hollisters."

"Totus dexter," Robert said, raising his finger.

"What?"

He grinned. "That's what a fellow in my Latin class always says. It means 'all right.' " He took some gold coins from his pocket and handed them to Susan.

"Fine. I guess we're all set, then. We'll go first thing in the morning. Oh!—which way is it to town?"

"Opposite the way we went to find the treasure," Victoria said. "Good night, sir, I hope you sleep well."

"Good night, sir," Robert said.

"Yes, good night, good night, thank you," Mr. Shaw said.

Robert closed the shutter of his bull's-eye, and he and the girls went outside. Victoria said, "Go on ahead, Bobbie, I want to speak with Sue privately a moment."

"Oh," she went on when Robert had left, "he *is* handsome! I do wish I could go with you when we buy his new clothes—we could make him so nobby! But, Sue . . . he seems—a little . . ."

"Unenthusiastic," Susan sighed. "I know. I could just choke him! I guess it's because he's having such a hard time believing what's happening. Grown-ups don't adjust very easily."

"No . . . Mama's going to be difficult too, I'm afraid. This afternoon I was sounding her out, very delicately, of course; and she as good as said that no man could ever interest her again. I think her spirits were dashed when she discovered the truth about Mr. Sweeney."

"That's understandable . . . Still, though, I don't think Daddy and I are up here for nothing. The witch gave me three trips on the elevator, after all; and so it couldn't have been *just* to chase Mr. Sweeney away, because we managed that on my first trip."

"That's so. We *are* dabbling in magic, aren't we? Oooh, it's so—shivery! I keep forgetting because it's all mixed up with real everyday things."

"Yes. Well, Daddy and your Mama can think what they want to think now; but I'm sure that when they meet each other, things will begin to happen. I wish I knew what time we'll be ready, but it'll all depend on how long we're in town. Could you just keep a lookout, and come outside when you see me?"

"Yes! And then when we've all had a chance to become acquainted, we'll persuade Mama to come out and meet the nice gentleman and his lovely daughter—"

"Oh, foo!" Susan said, giving Victoria a little push.

"And then as you said, things will begin to happen! Oh, I declare, I'm not going to be able to sleep a *wink* tonight!"

ᣞᣞᣞᣞ 4. A FAMILIAR FACE ᣞᣞᣞᣞ

. . . didn't sleep either, but later we took a nap on the way in. Daddy got a whole new outfit and looks very "nobby" as Vicky would say. An awful thing almost happened while we were waiting at the railroad station . . .

They were comfortable enough in the stable. Blankets and pillows had been smuggled in during the day by Robert, to spread over the straw. It was dark and quiet and warm. But they couldn't sleep.

Mr. Shaw shifted, and sighed, and shifted, and

yawned, and shifted again. Susan lay staring into the dark, feeling as though she were stuck on an emotional rollercoaster. Everything was going to fail. Everything was going to go like a dream. It would be a flop. It would be lovely . . . She chewed her knuckle until it was sore.

They started as a nearby rooster raucously predicted daybreak. Already? Yes, the stars were growing dim. A bird began to carol. Above her head the swallows stirred and squeaked in their nest.

Ah, well. They had to be gone before anyone else was up, and since they couldn't sleep anyway . . . "Come on, Daddy," she sighed. "Time to go."

He got up with a groan. Stiff-legged and yawning, they skirted the house, reached the dusty lane, and began to plod town-ward.

"That's Hollisters'," she murmured. "That's where we'll be staying." Mr. Shaw took a brief look and grunted. She could not feel any enthusiasm herself at the moment. The house looked dingy and forlorn next to the grandeur of the Walkers'.

They trudged about a mile in glum silence. The unfolding glory of sunrise only hurt their eyes. They were city people, unused to walking, and their legs quickly wearied. Susan's recently-sprained ankle throbbed. When they reached a little wooden bridge over a stream, Mr. Shaw leaned on the rail and croaked, "I need a rest." They stumbled down the bank to the water's edge and bathed their eyes. The buttercup-spangled grass on the bank was thick and soft. They sank down on it. The stream murmured over its pebbles; heat gathered in the air. They slept.

The sun was high overhead when they woke again. They splashed water on their faces and looked about them with revived spirits. "First good sleep I've had in several days," Mr. Shaw remarked. "I'm hungry!" she said. "Are you?" He clutched his midriff and groaned. "Come on," she cried, jumping up, "let's get to town quick and have something to eat! Oh, goodness, what a mess we are!" She began to brush bits of straw and grass from Mr. Shaw's rumpled clothes. Of course she had forgotten to bring a comb. Her father was going to need a shave soon, but neither of them had thought about bringing a razor. How could she have spent so much time considering the right kind of diary, and none at all thinking about necessities like combs and razors? They were going to have to outfit themselves from the ground up!

"Best foot forward!" Mr. Shaw said, and they set off again.

The first house appeared around a bend in the road, and beyond it a scattering of others. And now there were people ahead. Mr. Shaw stared. Susan found that she was staring too; she wasn't as used to nineteenth-century dress as she thought. "It's real, Daddy," she murmured, more to reassure herself than him. Her eyes darted everywhere: she was taking a crash course in contemporary fashions. 'I'll have to get a bonnet,' she thought.

The road turned into a tunnel under a vault of elms, and led them to the town square. "Can't be real," Mr. Shaw murmured; "must be a big movie set." There were formal rosebeds, a white bandstand as decorated as a wedding cake, some cannons on stone pedestals, a fountain, wooden plank sidewalks, stone hitching posts with iron rings.

A mouthwatering smell led them across the square to a bakery, where they bought half a dozen doughnuts. Munching these, they ambled along the plank sidewalk past a bank, a hardware store, a saloon, an aromatic livery stable, a carriage-maker's shop, and so on around two sides of the square until they came to Bardwell's Haberdashers and Gents' Outfitters.

"What is it I'm supposed to get, now?" Mr. Shaw asked.

Susan had drawn some conclusions from her crash course in styles. "Everything," she said firmly.

They went in. A young man with crisply-curled blond hair bounded forward with a glad cry of "Yes, sir!"

Mr. Shaw cleared his throat. "Ah . . . a new suit—"

The clerk looked Mr. Shaw up and down with an expert flick of his eyes. A puzzled look came over his face. Susan saw that it was time to clarify matters.

"My father and I have just returned from abroad," she said. "From . . . Prussia. Now that we're back, we think American clothing would be more suitable."

"*Of* course!" cried the clerk, his expression clearing at once. "You've certainly come to the right establishment, sir, if I may say so. Let me show you a cut, sir, that is highly recommended among the better element in these parts."

After a good deal of picking and choosing, Mr. Shaw was outfitted in a fawn-colored checked suit; a cream-colored waistcoat with gold buttons; a snowy shirt with a stand-up collar; a rich maroon cravat; and a straw hat. The clerk was entranced. "Capital, sir!" he cried. "Why, I guess the best concern in the city couldn't turn you out any better. But might I say, sir, that those, ah, Prooshian, ah, slippers—" He frowned at Mr. Shaw's twentieth-century shoes. "May I sud-gest, sir, that the bootmakers across the square, Jackson and Son, can furnish the genuine American article?"

"You do look marvelous, Daddy," Susan said as they

36

came out into the sunlight again. "So young and elegant. And now for the genuine American article!"

Leaving him at the bootmakers', she hurried around the shops until she had acquired a blue bonnet and a tortoise-shell comb for herself, shaving equipment for her father, and toothbrushes for both of them. These purchases, on top of Mr. Shaw's clothes and boots, reduced their funds to a few dollars. Susan looked down at her —Victoria's—dress and sighed. She had hoped . . .

Ah, well—maybe Vicky could come back to town with her tomorrow and help her choose a whole wardrobe. They would have a lovely time of it together . . .

Jim Perkins was nowhere in sight at the railroad station.

"He's at a business meetin'," the ticket-seller told them, giving Mr. Shaw a solemn wink. "Next train's due in five minutes; guess he'll be on hand for that—if he ain't been *liquidated.*" They sat down outside the station-house on a green bench. Mr. Shaw suddenly looked happy. "I just thought!" he said. "It's going to be a steam locomotive! It'll have to be if we're really . . . here. Wow! I haven't seen one since I was a kid." Susan had never seen one at all.

The station began to come alive. Wheels and hooves could be heard on the other side of the building; there were voices in the waiting room; people began to stroll up and down on the platform. Then the faraway sound of the whistle, like the one Susan had heard on her first night in this century; bustling sounds from the baggage shed; horses whickering and stamping out front. Then the locomotive was bearing down on them, black and smoky, filling the air with its hissing and the rumble of steel wheels on steel rails and the *ping* of its boiler. Mr. Shaw's eyes shone. Susan, feeling a mixture of fright and excitement, grabbed his sleeve and shouted, "Oh, Daddy, let's go somewhere on a train as soon as we can!" People began to move toward the cars. Among them she noticed a man who wore a derby tilted to reveal a wave of shining black hair, whose mustache was trimmed as if with a ruler, whose white hand fastidiously held a cigar . . .

Her heart turned over.

It was Mr. Sweeney.

He hadn't seen her. He was strolling toward one of the cars, valise in one hand, cigar in the other. He wouldn't see her if . . . There was a shout from the other end of the platform where men were handling the baggage. Mr. Sweeney's head began to turn. She doubled over and began to fiddle with her shoe. It was a buttoned one —she couldn't pretend to be tying it. Well, she was checking the buttons, then . . . Good grief, she wouldn't be able to straighten up again until the train was gone. Mr. Sweeney might happen to sit down by a window just opposite her . . . She was having trouble breathing.

"Daddy!" she whispered.

"What are you doing?" he asked.

"Daddy, stand in front of me! Bend over and look at my shoe."

"What's the—?"

"*Please!*" she hissed. She heard him grunt, and his puzzled face came level with hers. "Between me and the train!" she said. "Pretend you're looking at something that I'm showing you on my shoe." Her eyes darted right and left under her lowered lids. She could no longer see Mr. Sweeney. Her father's troubled gaze searched her face. "What's this all about?" he murmured.

"It's Mr. Sweeney! Come closer. Keep looking down at my shoe—pretend there's a hole in it or something."

"Who?"

"That fortune-hunter who was after Mrs. Walker! The one we scared away!"

"Oh! Hey, my back's getting tired, can I—?"

"*Don't move!* Not till the train goes."

"But why? What can he do if he does see you?"

"I don't know, but I don't want to find out!"

At last the cry of " 'Board!" sounded, the bell began to ring, the engine huffed, wheels skreeked; and the Shaws straightened up, gasping for air like swimmers who have surfaced just in time.

⋯❦ 5. PLOTTING ❦⋯

> *. . . got to Hollisters' all right. We had*
> *lunch and Daddy took a nap. I went out and*
> *"met" Vicky and Bobbie, and we tried to*
> *make plans. The big problem was how to get*
> *Daddy and Mrs. Walker to meet a* second
> *time. Vicky decided she would have to do*
> *something improper and desperate . . .*

"Woulda been here sooner," Jim Perkins said, "but I had to see a feller." He lowered his voice. "Business praposition," he confided. The Shaws recoiled from a strong smell of beer.

"We're vacationing in the country," Susan said. "Do you know anyone nearby that offers room and board?"

"Eee-yep. Know a place that will meet your requirements in every par-tickler. Cool breezy location, a view equalled by no other in these parts, *and*—" he paused to worry at a twist of tobacco "—victuals of the highest class. Hollisters'. Where's yer baggage?"

There was a moment's pause. "Uh, it's coming later," Susan said.

"Mix-up at the other end," Mr. Shaw added. And to prevent any further discussion he thrust two quarters at Jim Perkins, said, "Up you go, my dear," handed Susan into the surrey, and got in himself.

Jim Perkins projected a stream of tobacco juice over the left front wheel, tilted the remains of a top hat forward at a desperate angle over his forehead, hunched over as if to meet the onslaught of a heavy wind, and flicked the reins. The horse broke into a creaking amble.

The Shaws leaned back with a sigh.

Mrs. Hollister, a faded, shy woman, said yes, she guessed they could have two rooms upstairs.

"Reckon I could pick up yer baggage when it gets in," Jim Perkins said.

"Ah—no," Mr. Shaw said. "Thank you, but it's taken care of."

"Wouldn't be no trouble—"

"Can we see our rooms, please?" Susan said. "Thank you, Mr. Perkins, goodbye," and they made their escape into the house.

The rooms were small and untidy and needed dusting. 'Wouldn't Mrs. Clutchett love to give this place a going-over!' Susan thought. At the sight of his bed, Mr. Shaw yawned and remarked that he didn't know which he wanted more, lunch or a nap. "How about both?" Susan suggested. Mrs. Hollister produced cold chicken and bread and butter, which they fell upon like wolves. Then Mr. Shaw went to his room, laid himself down with a groan, and fell asleep.

Susan was too keyed up even to consider a nap. A ricketty little writing desk by one of the windows in her room reminded her of something. She sat down and brought her diary up to date, scribbling fast to get everything in, and glancing outside every few minutes to see if Victoria or Robert were about.

As soon as she was through, she ran outside. For the first time since her adventures had begun she could appear in full sight of the Walkers' house without worrying about being seen. She hurried toward the hedge that separated the two properties, muttering to herself, "Come on, you two, we're supposed to—oops!" She slowed down, remembering that she and the Walker children were "meeting" for the first time.

Ah, here they were!

She gave them a grave look over the privet, and said in Deportment Class tones, "How do you do? What a lovely house you live in!"

"Why, thank you," Victoria answered in similar tones. "I don't believe I've seen you before. Are you taking the air in this vicinity?"

Robert's face was twitching. Susan and Victoria, despite heroic efforts, burst into giggles.

"It's totus dexter," Robert laughed. "No one's watching. Come on over, Sue—we've met now. There's a place up here where you can go through the hedge."

"Let's sit in the swing," Victoria said.

In the Walkers' back yard, under a weeping willow's cascade of foliage, was a wooden swing—the kind with two facing seats and a floor, suspended in a frame. Susan was enchanted by it. She sat opposite the Walkers and watched dragonflies quartering the pond nearby. Robert pushed on the floor and started them swinging.

"Did everything go all right?" Victoria asked.

"Oh, yes, we got Daddy a jazzy suit—oh, pardon me, I guess I mean nobby—and he looks just marvelous, and then we went to the station and oh my goodness! I thought I'd faint—there was Mr. Sweeney!"

They looked at her with startled faces.

"Oh, it's all right, he didn't see *me*. I ducked down and Daddy stood in front of me. But I wanted to go right through the floor."

"But it's been—" Robert ticked off his fingers "—gosh! It's been four days since we chased him away. I wonder why he stayed in town so long?"

"He was getting on the train, anyway," Susan said. "If he'd been getting *off* we might have something to worry about. Now we know he's really gone . . . Well!

Daddy's taking a nap. I'm kind of worried about him. He has this funny look as though he doesn't believe anything that's happening. Or as though it's happening to somebody else . . . He's in a better mood now, but he's just not involved yet. How're things at your end?"

"Oh, Mama's involved, all right," Robert said, frowning. "That's our trouble—she believes everything that's happened. It's fixed in her mind that we're ruined."

"She's going through her papers and making lists of things that have to be done," Victoria added. "She's really wonderful, you know—so brave and—and resolute. But I declare, she's carrying it too far. Maggie isn't making anything easier, either; she's looking glum and muttering about how her second sight is bothering her. Only she won't say how."

"Second sight?"

"Yes. She claims that she sees—oh, visions. Remember I told you that once she saw her brother seven months after he'd been drowned? Anyway, she's hinting that something dreadful is going to happen soon. She says," Victoria lowered her voice, "she says that she's seen a sign."

"What kind of a sign?"

"She won't tell us. All she'll say is, 'I wouldn't be wantin' to make your flesh creep!' "

"Oh, foo!" Susan said, trying to ignore the little shiver that had run down her spine.

"Something dreadful *is* going to happen," Robert said. "You don't need second sight to know it, either. Cousin Jane arrives tomorrow on the one-thirty-seven."

They all sighed.

"Well," Susan said, "we'll just have to get Daddy and your Mama together as many times as we can before that. Now, what I'm going to do in a little while is this:

when Daddy wakes up, we're going for a walk and I'm going to show him the treasure—"

"We really ought to move the treasure to a safer place," Robert interrupted.

"We will, when there's time. But I want to show him now—it might jolt a little belief into him. And anyway, we need some more money for current expenses. Then we'll walk back by your house. Can you bring your Mama out then?"

"We'll try," Victoria said. "It would be easier if she weren't so busy and preoccupied."

"Trust us, Sue," Robert said. "We'll have her out if we have to *dragoon* her into it."

"Fine! Now, just in case they need a little more encouragement, how can we get them together this evening?"

Victoria gave her a worried look. "That's the trouble, Sue. It will be up to your Papa to make the next move, but it would be *much* too hasty of him to call that soon."

"Oh. Well, how about tomorrow morning?"

Victoria began to twist her hands. "Well, you see, Sue, it's not that Mama is stuffy, because she isn't; but she does believe in propriety, and—well, the proper time for making a call is between two and five in the afternoon."

"Oh, good grief, Vick! We don't have *time* to be proper!"

"I know, Sue. But on the other hand, if we allow your Papa to commit social blunders, Mama will be put off— and then we'll lose even more time."

"I've got it!" Robert said. "Maybe we can arrange an accidental meeting. Or an emergency. Nobody bothers about what's proper in an emergency."

"What kind of emergency?" Susan asked.

"Something dangerous that would throw them to-

44

gether. Something dire."

"Mmmm!" Victoria said. A dreamy smile came across her face. "Oh, wouldn't it be splendid if we were picnicking somewhere and a dreadful tempest suddenly sprang up and flood waters were rising by the minute and your Papa dashed up on a wild-eyed steed crying 'By the Heavens, Madame, there is not a second to spare!' and swept Mama up in his—"

"Vi-ick!" Robert protested.

"And what would be wrong with that, you unfeeling brute?"

"Come on," Susan said. "It has to be something that can really happen. That we can *make* happen. Think!"

They thought.

But nothing seemed workable. An accidental meeting could only happen if Mrs. Walker were out-of-doors for some reason. Victoria and Robert agreed that tearing her away from her work once would be hard enough; twice would be impossible without some compelling excuse. Such as? Well . . . After a long silence Robert suggested a fire in the stable. The girls shuddered—much too dangerous. Victoria came back to her wild-eyed steed; it was hard to discard something so attractive. In novels, the hero and heroine were frequently brought together by a runaway horse. Imagine Mr. Shaw being thrown from his panic-stricken mount right in front of the house, and Mama rushing out to kneel by his insensible form— "Daddy doesn't know how to ride, he wouldn't even get on a horse," Susan said. Another long silence. Then Robert offered himself as sacrificial victim. He could fall out of a tree. Mr. Shaw, who would just happen to be passing by at that moment, could carry him into the house.

"That would be pretty good, actually," Susan said. "If

45

you didn't hurt yourself."

"Oh, I'd have to hurt myself, Sue. Then your Papa could call as often as he liked, to see how I was mending."

"No," Victoria said, "that would just be too hard on poor Mama, to have you hurt on top of everything else."

Once again, a long silence, broken only by a little crunching noise each time the swing passed a certain spot.

At last Victoria said, with an expression of desperate resolve, "I—I believe it is going to be up to me."

"What? What?" Susan and Robert asked.

"I'm going to force Mama's hand during the first meeting. I'm going to suggest that we invite you and your Papa over this very evening for—oh, I don't know what, I'll think of something. I'll suggest it while we're all talking together, so it will be very awkward for Mama to say no. Too awkward, I hope . . . You'll have to second me, Bobbie."

Robert nodded with a troubled look. "Totus dexter. But there'll probably be a blow-up afterwards."

"I know," Victoria said, shivering. "It *is* a dreadfully ill-bred thing to do, and she'll be so vexed . . . I wouldn't do it under any other circumstances in the world!"

"And if that doesn't work?" Susan said, chewing her knuckle.

Victoria threw up her hands. "Oh, goodness!" she cried. "I don't know. Perhaps we'll all have to fall out of a tree!"

⚜ 6. MEETING ⚜

> *. . . we went to see the treasure. And then came the Big Event. It was* terrible—*he looked at her and she looked at him and—nothing! They were going to say goodbye again almost right away, but Vicky forced Mrs. Walker's hand and I had to force Daddy's so we could get them together again next morning. I thought the situation was saved, only it wasn't . . .*

Susan waited, fidgeting, for her father to wake up. He lay on his back, breathing tranquilly, his hands folded over the gold buttons of his waistcoat. He looked as though he could sleep that way for hours. She knew he needed it; but on the other hand, here was the afternoon wearing away, and the great encounter—the whole point of being here, after all—hadn't happened yet . . . Finally she could stand it no longer, and shook him awake.

"Come on, Daddy. I want to show you something. Remember I told you you were going to be rich? Now I'm going to prove it!"

For the second time that day they set off down the road—but this time in the opposite direction.

"Now we can see the Walkers' house from the front," she said. "Isn't it gorgeous? Don't you love those iron stags in the yard?"

"Mmm," he said. "Pretty impressive. When do I meet Mrs. Walker?"

She glanced at him to see how he meant this. There

was no eagerness in his face—he just wanted to know. She sighed and said, "Soon now. Bobbie and Vicky are going to bring her out when they see us coming back."

They walked on.

"Daddy," she said after a while, "if you happened to be going along this road by yourself, would it ever occur to you that there was a treasure hidden somewhere along here?"

"Nope."

"Here, stop. Look around, now. If you *did* suspect a treasure, would you know where to look? Do you see anything unusual?"

"Can't say that I do," Mr. Shaw said after a close scrutiny of both sides of the road. "Looks to me like plain ordinary bushes along a fence."

She smiled with relief. "It's safe as a bank!" she said. "I don't know what Bobbie's so worried about. See that dead stick with the fork at the end? That's the mark." She glanced up and down the road to make sure it was deserted, and said, "Are you seeking your fortune, Mr. Shaw? Try looking here."

They crept on their hands and knees under a tunnel of arching canes. Here it was—she could tell by the feel. "Look!" she said. She brushed away a carpet of dead leaves to reveal the coarse weave of gunny sacking, and pulled aside a fold of the cloth.

"Holy smoke!" Mr. Shaw said.

"Feel it! Isn't it a marvelous sensation?"

They lifted handfuls of gold coins and let them slither through their fingers.

"Good night!" Mr. Shaw murmured. "Is this *real*?"

"Oh, Daddy, you're enough to drive me to distraction! Can't you *feel* what's real?"

"Okay, chick, don't bite my head off. I handle thousands of dollars a week, you know—only it's all pieces of paper and numbers. This— Is it really ours?"

"Yes. Yours. Here, put these in your pocket for—for whatever we might need them for."

She covered up the hoard again, and they backed out of the tunnel.

"All right! Or 'totus dexter', as Bobbie says. Now to meet Mrs. Walker! Ready?"

"I guess."

She brushed a few bits of leaf from his coat, and straightened his cravat. "Remember, you're wearing a hat," she warned. "You're supposed to lift it when you're introduced."

"Right." He practiced a few times. "What am I supposed to say, anyway?"

"Oh, you're not *supposed* to say anything—you're not speaking lines. You're just a person meeting another person—all you do is talk together. I'll help you if you get stuck."

They dawdled along the whole width of the Walker property without any sign of life from the house. 'Oh, good grief!' Susan thought, applying her teeth to her knuckle, 'something's gone wrong.' She steered her father into the Hollisters' yard, and they sauntered along the hedge that divided the two properties. 'Anyway,' she thought, 'we can walk back and forth here as much as we want. We're here to take the air, after all.'

And then, oh, relief!—the front door of the Walkers' house opened, and here came Mrs. Walker at last, being herded across the lawn by her children. 'Oh,' Susan thought, her heart beating high, 'how could Daddy *possibly* not fall in love with her?' For Mrs. Walker was even more lovely than she had remembered. She was wearing a simple white muslin dress. Her chestnut hair gleamed in the sunlight. There were shadows under her eyes—no one was sleeping well these days!—but they added to her beauty rather than detracted from it. Susan gave her father a quick glance. Good!—she could see that he was favorably impressed.

"Susan!" Victoria called out. "How nice to see you again so soon!"

"Hello, Victoria, hello, Robert! Papa and I are taking a stroll. Papa, these are the new friends I told you about: Victoria Walker and her brother Robert."

"Delighted to meet you, Mr. Shaw," Victoria said, with only a slight touch of Deportment Class. "May I introduce you to our mother? This is Mr. Shaw, Mama."

"How do you do, Mr. Shaw."

"Pleased to meet you, Mrs. Walker," and 'Oh, good for you, Daddy!' Susan thought as he lifted his hat and inclined his head with as much ease as if he'd been doing it all his life.

"And his daughter, Susan."

"How do you do, Susan," Mrs. Walker said, turning to her with such a lovely little smile that she thought she would melt into the ground with pleasure.

There was a moment of silence. They were all looking at Mr. Shaw. He flushed, but made a gallant try. "The, ah, weather was so beautiful we had to come out and— look at the flowers and so forth."

"Yes," Mrs. Walker said, looking about and breathing deeply, "it is beautiful, isn't it? I've been so busy lately that I've quite neglected the out-of-doors. Why, I might have missed today's sunshine altogether if my children hadn't insisted on my coming out."

"We, ah," Mr. Shaw plowed ahead, "we've been, ah, walking up the road—" He froze, then shot a desperate glance at Susan.

"We've been admiring the countryside," Susan said. "Such lovely flowers and birds."

"I'm so glad you are enjoying it. I understand that you will be vacationing here for a while?"

"Well, actually," Mr. Shaw said, "I don't think we can—"

"Our plans are flexible," Susan interrupted. Good grief, did he really mean what he had started to say? She hurried on: "We find life in the city very tiring—indeed, there are days when I can hardly stand it. Coming to the country is like coming to a whole new world."

"Yes—the loveliest of all worlds," Mrs. Walker said, looking around her again. Her face grew sad, and her eyes brightened with tears. 'Oh, you dumb cluck!' Susan raged at herself. 'That was the wrong thing to say. She thinks she has to lose all this and go live in the city.'

Mrs. Walker's back stiffened, and she turned again to the Shaws with her face composed. "Forgive me, Mr. Shaw. You find us at a difficult moment, I'm afraid. Our circumstances have altered, and we are all a little upset."

"Oh. I'm sorry," Mr. Shaw said. "If there's any way I can help—"

"Thank you, no. I appreciate your concern, but we have matters well in hand, and assistance will be arriving soon . . . Well, I do hope you have a pleasant vacation, and that you may go back to the city refreshed. It was a pleasure to meet you, Mr. Shaw; and you too, Susan."

'No, wait!' Susan thought in a panic. 'We can't say goodbye now! *Nothing's happened yet!*' But Mrs. Walker was turning to go, her father was saying "My pleasure," and lifting his hand to tip his hat again . . .

Susan shot a despairing glance at Victoria.

Victoria's face turned scarlet. She said, "M-Mama?" It came out in a strangled bleat.

"Yes, dear?"

"Could we not—invite—Mr. Shaw and Susan over this evening—to—to—to look at our magic lantern pictures?"

"Oh, yes, Mama!" Robert put in with feverish brightness. "I believe Susan told us that Mr. Shaw was in the Army. Perhaps he'd like to see my views of the Great Battlefields of Europe!"

"*Children!*" Mrs. Walker froze for an instant, then turned back to the Shaws. Her cheeks were pink. "Do please forgive my unruly brood, Mr. Shaw! They sometimes allow their impetuousness to overcome their good breeding."

"Oh, I understand," Mr. Shaw said, smiling. "Susan sometimes does the same. *I* know what it is to be a parent."

She gave him a grateful smile and said, "Children, if you wish to see more of Susan, you have my permission; provided, of course, that she has her Papa's permission to see more of you."

"Oh, absolutely," Mr. Shaw said.

"Mama," Victoria said, turning if possible even redder than before, "could we—invite them—tomorrow morning for—for—?"

"For tea?" Robert croaked.

Mrs. Walker was so thunderstruck that she seemed for an instant to forget the Shaws. "*Tea?*" she asked. "In the *morning?*"

"Cousin Jane will be here in the afternoon, Mama," Robert faltered, "and then . . ."

Victoria burst into tears. "Oh, Mama," she sobbed, "I know it's dreadfully improper, but our poor dear house *deserves* to have one more happy scene in it before we—before we have to—oh, oh, oh, oh!"

"There, there," Mrs. Walker murmured. She put her arms around Victoria. Her own eyes were brimming again. "I seem to have to ask your forgiveness very often, Mr. Shaw! My daughter is strongly attached to our house, and—well, you see, we are forced to give it up."

"Oh!" Susan cried. "How dreadful for you. I'm so sorry."

Mr. Shaw murmured, and looked at Mrs. Walker with an expression of troubled concern.

"I believe," Victoria hiccupped, "that I could—rest content if we could—offer the hospitality of our dear house—once more before we—leave it forever."

A musing look came over Mrs. Walker's face. "Yes," she said, half to herself, "we have been very happy in our house . . . Perhaps we *could* express our gratitude by—" She gave a wry little smile. "Mr. Shaw, Susan, pray do not think us absurd or forward. If you can countenance the impropriety of it, please come and take tea with us tomorrow morning. The afternoon, I'm afraid, will be taken up with business. Shall we say ten-thirty? Think of it as a kindness to us—helping us to say goodbye."

"I'm awfully sorry about your house," Mr. Shaw said. "It must be a terrible blow. And I appreciate your very kind invitation. But the fact is—"

Good heavens—*he was going to refuse!* She had to act fast.

"Oh, we'd just love to come!" Susan cried. Hoping that the hedge would hide the gesture from Mrs. Walker, she reached out with her foot and pressed down hard on her father's toe. "I don't think it's absurd or improper or anything like that."

"But really," Mr. Shaw said, sliding his foot out from under hers, "I'm afraid—"

He was going to ruin everything! She couldn't let him do it.

She screamed.

They all jumped and looked at her with startled faces. She twisted her mouth into a grimace of pain, clutched her knee in both hands, and began to hop backwards. "Yellow jackets!" she shrieked. "Look out!"

She could see understanding flash into Robert's face. "Great Caesar!" he cried. "They're swarming in the hedge! Run, Mama! Run, Vick!"

Susan grabbed her father's hand and yelled, "Run, Daddy!"

As the Shaws and the Walkers fled in opposite directions, Victoria called back over her shoulder, "Ten-thirty tomorrow morning!" and Susan answered, "We'll be there!"

The Shaws came to rest on the Hollisters' veranda.

"Good night!" Mr. Shaw panted. "We'd better get a cold wet cloth. Does it hurt bad?"

"Hurts," she said, bending over and hugging her imaginary sting. She was having trouble suppressing a triumphant giggle. "It's—hoo!—all right, Daddy, really. I can stand it."

"What a devil of a time for yellow jackets to start acting up! I was just about to turn down her invitation."

"Why?"

"Because we can't accept it, that's why. We're going to have to send her a note, or go back over and make our apologies."

She pretended amazement, but her heart was contracting with dread. "Why can't we accept it?"

"We're not going to be here."

"But—"

"No ifs, ands or buts. We're going back to the twentieth century as soon as we can possibly get to the elevator. Tonight."

⊰ 7. MR. HOLLISTER DISCOURSES ⊱

. . . had a discussion. Daddy was right in a way—he had done what he had said he'd do, and since Mrs. Walker hadn't bowled him over, why shouldn't we go back? I could tell, though, that all we needed was a little more time. Mr. Hollister gave us the time, but he almost killed us doing it . . .

"Oh, Daddy," she moaned.

"Now, look here, chick," Mr. Shaw said, "it's time we got things straightened out." He sat down on the veranda steps, took off his hat, and mopped his brow. "I've been very patient with you so far . . . We had a bargain, remember?"

She had sunk down on the steps beside him. She nodded her head, too miserable to speak.

"Your part of the bargain was that you'd accept some professional help as soon as I could get an appointment. Well, maybe we can forget that. My part of the bargain was that I agreed to come up the elevator with you in costume to meet a certain lady. And I've done it. I did *not* agree to lose another night's sleep and walk my legs off and go through a lot of folderol with new clothes and hide-and-seek at the railroad station and so forth and so on. But I've done all that too. Now I want to go back."

Susan shook herself free of the numbness that was threatening to settle over her.

"Daddy," she said, "when you saw Mrs. Walker, didn't —didn't anything happen? Didn't you *feel* anything?"

"Well, you were right about her—she is a beautiful woman. I felt the usual amount of interest and attraction that I feel when I'm talking to a beautiful woman."

"Was that all?"

"Well, I felt admiration for her—I think she's very gallant. I felt sorry for her because she's feeling bad. I felt—oh, well, I'll be honest with you. What I was feeling most of all was, 'I'll be glad when this is over.' "

"Oh . . ."

"Oh, Susie, you look so crushed! Did you really think I was just going to up and fall in love? Like that?" He snapped his fingers.

She gulped and nodded.

"You've been watching too many movies on that television set, chick. That's not the way things happen in real life."

"But they could happen that way, couldn't they?" she insisted.

"Oh, I guess so . . . I'll concede the point that I could possibly fall in love with her. She *is* gallant and beautiful and appealing, and if she belonged to my own time, I— But that's the thing right there, Susie: time. You and I belong to the twentieth century, not here."

"Do you really *like* the twentieth century, Daddy?"

"It's not a question of whether I like it or not. It's our time. It's our place. It's where we know what to do and what to say. It's where your school is and where my job is."

"Oh, school!" she snorted, waving her hand. "And you're not all that crazy about your job, either. Are you?"

"Well, it's not the most exciting job in the world, no. But I know how to do it, and a lot of people rely on me to do it, and I do it well."

"Oh, Daddy . . ."

"I know, I know," he said with a rueful little laugh. "It must sound very uninspiring . . . I guess it's the difference between being young and being grown up. When you're young, you think everything you want to happen, will. When you're grown up you learn to accept the fact that most of it won't. I'm sorry that's the way it is, but it is."

"But, Daddy, if—"

"So to get back where we started from: we had a bargain. I've fulfilled my part of it. As soon as we can get back to the elevator tonight we're going home."

Well, maybe he thought the subject was closed; but as far as she was concerned, it wasn't. She had recovered from the initial shock by now, and hope was beginning to reassert itself. He had said so many things that hope could fasten on! "A beautiful woman," he had admitted without hesitation. "Gallant," he had said. "Very appealing. I could very possibly fall in love with her . . ." His exact words!—well, almost exact. 'Good grief!' she thought, 'he's right on the edge already. He's not willing to recognize it, that's the trouble. Why, I bet the real reason he's so eager to get back is because he's running away! He's making up all those fuddy-duddy excuses about school and his job and "our time" because he's *afraid* of falling in love . . . Oh, there just has to be a way to keep him here a little longer, so things can

57

have time to develop!'

There was.

She almost fell off the steps as the solution hit her. It was so simple and so foolproof! They couldn't go back to the twentieth century if the doors of the Walkers' house were locked. All it required was a word to Victoria or Robert . . . So they *would* be here tomorrow, after all; and being here, they could accept Mrs. Walker's invitation to tea; and for an hour at least (maybe more!) Mrs. Walker's beauty and gallantry and appeal could make headway against her father's reluctance. And if still *more* time were needed—well, she and Victoria and Robert would think of something.

A lathered horse appeared out on the road, drawing a dilapidated buggy. It turned in through the gate and headed directly toward them. The driver had a familiar appearance.

"It's Uncle Sam, right out of a cartoon!" Mr. Shaw said in a low voice. "A seedy Uncle Sam." The resemblance was so comic that Susan burst into giggles.

Mrs. Hollister emerged from the house, wiping her hands on her apron. "There's the mister," she murmured.

He drew up by the veranda, threw the reins around the stone hitching post, and came toward them, wagging his grey goatee and emitting loud nasal sounds.

"These're the new boarders, Hiram," Mrs. Hollister mumbled.

"N-yas!" Mr. Hollister brayed, displaying large horsey teeth and bearing down on the Shaws with his hand extended.

"Mr. Shaw," Mrs. Hollister murmured at the ceiling. "Miss Shaw."

"A very rare and welcome privilege, sir! And this little lady!" Mr. Hollister's voice dropped four whole tones. He whipped off his mangy stove-pipe hat, pressed it against the frayed edging and food spots on his waistcoat, bowed over it and intoned, "A radiant vision of—ha—budding young womanhood."

Susan curtseyed. Her face was red with the effort of keeping her embarrassed laughter down.

Mr. Hollister's voice resumed its original pitch. "I sincerely hope and trust, sir, that you propose to stop in these parts for an extensive length of time."

"I don't know," Mr. Shaw said. "Probably not very long. I—"

"Grieved to hear it, sir, acutely grieved. Let me entertain the idea, sir, that further acquaintance with this vicinity will lead you to revise your plans. I believe there is more opportunity here, sir, then is to be found anywhere in these United States. Why, the very air you are now breathing, sir—" his voice performed its four-tone plunge "—the—ha—salubricity of this air, sir, is a matter of record at the State capitol itself. Fact. The fertility of the soil hereabouts—"

"Hiram," Mrs. Hollister murmured. "Supper."

"N-yas. *If* you will pardon me for a brief interim, sir." Wagging his goatee and braying through his nose, Mr. Hollister went off to stable his horse.

"If you want to wash up," Mrs. Hollister mumbled. The Shaws followed her to a lean-to shed in back of the house, where they washed their hands with yellow soap under a pump, and tried to dry them on a dank roller towel. 'I'll have to see Vicky and Bobbie right after dinner about locking up,' Susan thought. She felt a twinge of conscience. Was it right to prevent their return? Her father *had* done everything she had asked . . . Ugh, this towel! She dropped it, and wiped her hands on her dress. 'It's only for one more day,' she promised that nagging voice within. 'Just to make sure.'

Dinner was a plentiful amount of roast beef, potatoes, onions and gravy, all glistening with grease. In a while Mr. Hollister returned, smelling very horsey and braying. He took up his oration exactly where he had left off.

"The fertility of the soil in these parts, sir, is nothing short of phenomenal. A bumper crop is guaranteed each season. The water, sir, has a balanced mineral content that ensures the health of man and beast. The local climate is equalled by none. In short, sir, the spot has been chosen by—ha—Providence. A man of means, sir, could do no better than to invest those means right here. And consider this, sir." His voice dropped. "Progress, sir. Growth." He pointed a knobby index finger over his left shoulder. "The city, sir, is extending its enriching boundaries in this direction. If the currency question, sir, were to be settled as every right-thinking citizen of this Republic knows it should be settled—" He suddenly paused with upraised hand. "But perhaps, sir, I am treading on delicate ground. May I ask, sir, where your—ha—political sympathies lie?"

"Now, Hiram," Mrs. Hollister murmured.

Mr. Shaw roused himself. "Well, ah," he said. He looked at Susan. She looked back. He shrugged. "Last election I voted Democratic, for all the good it did me."

"N-yas!" Mr. Hollister brayed. "I had only to look at you, sir, to divine that you were a man of sound politics! The name of Democrat may have its ups and downs, sir, but show me a man that calls himself Republican, and I'll show you either a misguided fool or a scoundrel. The Republican machine, sir—"

"Now, Hiram."

"—is the most devilish engine ever constructed for the oppression of mankind. The vast majority of the populace of this continent groans under its yoke, sir, while a handful of thieves and parasites battens on the lifeblood of—"

The Shaws' eyes glazed. Their dinner settled heavily in their stomachs; a foggy torpor overcame their spirits. In some rapidly dimming corner of her mind Susan recalled that there was something she wanted to do after dinner, but what it was she could no longer remember. Mr. Hollister contrived, without a second's interruption in the flood of words, to light a powerful stogie. Its fumes finally roused them sufficiently to push back from the table and stagger out to the veranda. He pursued them, relentlessly braying. They fell into a prolonged stupor, from which Mr. Shaw at last rescued them only by a superhuman recovery of will.

"Bedtime," he mumbled, struggling to his feet like a man who has been repeatedly knocked down with a club.

"One more point, sir," Mr. Hollister trumpeted, thrusting the glowing tip of his third cigar at them through the dark. "The recent merger of the telegraph companies is but one more sinister straw in the wind. You may count on it, sir, that the foul hand of the Republican machine was tightly grasping the controls. I have no hesitation in asserting—"

"Goo'night," Mr. Shaw croaked. He grabbed Susan's hand and pulled her from her wicker chair. Numbly they crawled up the stairs. Mr. Hollister's denunciation flowed on behind them, unabated.

"Remember," Mr. Shaw muttered thickly, nodding in the direction of the Walkers' house.

"Mm-mm," she murmured, feeling too bludgeoned to know whether she was saying yes or no.

They crawled into their respective beds. 'Daddy can wake us up,' she thought, falling instantly asleep. After an interval of darkness she found herself in the elevator with him, going down, sinking away from the ruin of her hopes. She raised her face to cry out. The light bulb in the ceiling blazed so brightly that she had to throw her hand up to cover her eyes. The movement woke her up. Her room was golden with sunshine, and outside a rooster shouted that she had been reprieved.

⊰ 8. SINGULAR BEHAVIOR OF MAGGIE ⊱

> . . . *saved for another day, and I thought it was a good omen. Daddy said yes we could go to the Walkers' tea now, but we would take the elevator first chance we got. I decided not to let there be a chance. We went over at 10:30. Vicky and Bobbie opened the door and the minute I saw them I knew something awful had happened . . .*

"It's fate, Daddy! Suppose we *had* been able to stay awake last night until it was safe to take the elevator— think how worn out we'd be now! I'd be falling asleep in class, and you'd be making such awful mistakes at work that your company would lose thousands of dollars!"

He was not amused. But she was too happy to care. It did seem that fate was intervening in their favor, and if her father couldn't see it that way, it was because he hadn't realized yet what was good for him.

"Well, anyway," she went on, "since we are still here, and since we didn't get a chance to refuse Mrs. Walker's invitation, we might as well go there for tea, don't you think?"

"Yes," he answered, so readily that she was startled. Had he changed his mind? "And," he continued, "if there's any chance of getting to that elevator while we're there—any chance at all—we're going to grab it."

"Oh," she said.

"As a matter of fact, I don't see why we even have to wait for a chance. Why can't we just make our apologies and say goodbye and *go*?"

She was aghast. "You mean right in front of everybody?"

"Sure, why not? Robert and Victoria know all about it—they've seen it in operation, haven't they? They could explain it to Mrs. Walker. *We* could explain it to her, for that matter."

"Oh no!"

"Why not, for heaven's sake?"

"Be-be-because," she stammered. Her mind was racing to think of some way to cut off this dreadful line of reasoning. "Because . . . I mean we just *can't*. It's her house, and she—she . . . Would you really be cruel enough to give poor Mrs. Walker that kind of a shock? 'Oh, pardon us, Mrs. Walker, we have to go now,' and then a wall *in her own house* opens up and swallows us alive. That's what it would look like to her, even if we explained it to her. Why, Daddy, she's under such a strain already, something like that could drive her right over the edge!"

"Oh, all right, all right," he said, rubbing his face. "Not in front of her, then: I'm willing to spare her feelings. But if she leaves us to ourselves for any reason, or if we can think of any excuse to leave her—down we go!"

She sighed, hoping that he would take it as agreement on her part, and they were silent for a while. "We'd better get ready," she said at last. "Oh, I got you something yesterday, Daddy, let me show you." She went to her room and brought back the shaving things: a deadly-looking straight razor, a soap mug, a brush, and a honing strop. They were a great success, particularly the razor.

"Oh, wow, thank you, chick! This is really beautiful. My grandfather had one like this."

"Do you know how to use it?"

"Oh, I have a good idea—I used to watch Grandpa." He pinched his nose and twisted his mouth halfway around his face.

She giggled, and said, "I'll get some hot water."

Mrs. Hollister apologetically pointed out the kettle simmering on an enormous black range. On a nearby shelf a porcelain clock with cupids and roses painted on it said 9:23. Not much more than an hour until . . . 'Something's *got* to happen this time,' she thought.

She hurried back upstairs with the kettle, and they had a good morning wash-up. While Mr. Shaw plied his new razor, Susan went to her room, tore a piece of paper out of her diary, and wrote on it: "Don't let your Mama leave the room under *any circumstances*. This is *very important*." She folded it small and put it in her pocket. 'I'll just slip this to Vicky or Bobbie as we go in,' she thought. 'We are *not* going down that elevator until I'm convinced the whole thing is absolutely hopeless.'

"Only one nick!" Mr. Shaw announced. "Not so bad for a beginner, eh? Say, chick," he lowered his voice, "you didn't see anything of Uncle Sam Windbag downstairs, did you?"

"No. I think he's gone."

"He'd better be! I must say, though, he's as good as a handful of sleeping pills. I slept better last night than I have in years."

They went down to a welcome breakfast of ham, eggs, fried potatoes and biscuits.

At twenty-five minutes after ten they strolled over to the Walkers'. Susan drew the mild summer air deeply into her lungs. This was it! Her heart was beginning to thud, and she had to suppress a desire to bounce at her father's side like a rubber ball. Dignity, dignity! Bouncing could come later . . .

The double front doors were of varnished oak, with stained-glass windowpanes. The knocker was a feminine bronze hand delicately holding a ball between its thumb and two fingers. Susan lifted it and rapped once. There was a sudden murmur of voices within, a sharp exclamation, the sound of running feet. The door swung open to reveal the Walker children.

"Good morning, good morning!" the Shaws began, but their voices died at the sight of the stricken faces confronting them.

From inside the house an unfamiliar voice cried, "Robert! Victoria!"

65

"She's here!" Victoria mouthed. Aloud she said, in a Deportment Class voice that was badly cracked around the edges, "Oh, good morning, Mr. Shaw. Good morning, Miss Shaw. Won't you please come in?"

"Who?" Mr. Shaw said.

"Cousin Jane!" Victoria groaned in a whisper.

"But," Susan murmured, "I thought she wasn't—"

"She came by the eight-forty-seven instead of the afternoon train," Robert whispered. "We've been outflanked!"

"Really, Isabelle," the voice inside went on, "I am at a loss to understand this behavior in your children. You have a servant, I believe. It should be her duty to answer the door."

With despairing glances at their guests, the Walkers ushered them in and turned toward the parlor. Susan was so numb with apprehension that she forgot the note in her pocket. Her father seemed to have something stuck in his throat. Stiff-legged, they advanced to meet the owner of that voice.

She was sitting rigidly upright on the edge of a dark green plush sofa. Her eyes transfixed them—wintry grey eyes that glittered behind steel-rimmed pince-nez glasses. Her stout figure was dressed entirely in black. Her hair was black, too, drawn tightly into a bun.

Mrs. Walker, very pale but composed, also sitting stiffly upright on the edge of her chair, said in a low voice, "Ah, there you are! So nice to see you again. Mr. Shaw, I would like you to meet my cousin, Miss Clamp."

"A pleasure, Miss Clamp." He tentatively offered his hand and then dropped it again as Cousin Jane inclined her head a quarter of an inch forward and said, "How do you do." Her mouth tightened and her brows twitched together.

"Daddy!" Susan murmured out of the corner of her

mouth. "Hat!"

"Oh! Ahhrrrem! I, ah—" Mr. Shaw snatched his hat off, and turned red.

Mrs. Walker didn't seem to notice. She went on, "And this is Mr. Shaw's daughter, Susan. Susan and my two have become great friends."

Susan curtseyed. Cousin Jane said, "Indeed?" and gave her an arctic stare.

"Pray be seated," Mrs. Walker said. "Maggie will be in soon with the tea."

All the available chairs were in the line of fire of Cousin Jane's eyes. Aware that every movement was being watched, the Shaws and the Walker children sank into their seats.

"Do not loll, Victoria," Cousin Jane said after a moment of silence. "It is not only ill-bred, but also has a detrimental effect on one's carriage."

Victoria blushed and jerked rigidly upright. Susan felt her own spine stiffening. Mr. Shaw, meanwhile, was having trouble deciding what to do with his hat. He threw a quick questioning glance at Susan. She signalled back that she was as uncertain as he was. His chair had carved wooden arms; and after fumbling with his hat for a moment, he hung it on the end-knob of the left arm. Susan glanced at Cousin Jane, and saw her mouth and brows tightening again. 'Oh, good grief!' she groaned to herself; 'everything we do is going to be wrong . . .'

"Mr. Shaw!" Cousin Jane said. "You are vacationing in this vicinity, I believe."

"Yes, ma'am," Mr. Shaw said, jumping a little and knocking his hat to the floor. He bent over and picked it up again, turning redder than before.

"It's quite all right to leave your hat on the floor, Mr. Shaw," Mrs. Walker said with a faint but encouraging smile. Mr. Shaw, his face purple, laid his hat on the floor. He raised himself again to find everyone looking at him. "Beautiful day," he said, apparently squeezing the words past a grape-sized obstruction in his throat. "The *aherrrrem* sun—the sun's out."

"Yes!" Mrs. Walker said. "Such lovely weather lately. Early summer is one of my favorite times of year."

"Clement weather is never to be trusted," Cousin Jane said. "I expect it will rain soon.—Cease that fidgeting, Robert! Put both feet on the floor and keep your hands in your lap.—This area is noted for its high rainfall and the severity of its electrical storms. I wonder, Mr. Shaw, that you did not choose to vacation at the seaside or in the mountains. Most people resort to one or the other, I believe."

"Well, I, ah, *like* the country," Mr. Shaw said. "It's so restful and . . . quiet."

"There is a good deal of talk about the so-called virtues of country living," Cousin Jane said with a little sniff. "I believe it is sentimental twaddle. What is worse, it is pernicious twaddle. There is a dangerous relaxation of standards in the country which encourages bad manners in the young, and eccentricities in their elders."

Mrs. Walker turned a shade paler, but answered in a steady voice, "I realize that tea in the morning is— unusual, Cousin Jane. But the heart, after all, has its reasons that—"

"The heart, Isabelle, is the most unreliable organ in the human frame. Consulting it can lead only to sentimental excesses and improprieties—if not worse."

"Mama is not to be blamed, Cousin Jane," Victoria said in a voice so low that it was nearly a whisper. "It was really my idea."

"In-deed?" Cousin Jane slowly swiveled her head to-

68

ward Victoria, who, without relaxing her backbone or indeed moving a muscle, shrank. Susan felt her face growing warm with anger. Mr. Shaw cleared his throat loudly and said:

"Oh, come now, Miss Clamp, it wasn't such a horrendous idea! I think it was . . . charming."

Cousin Jane closed her eyes. "The whimsies of unformed minds may seem charming, Mr. Shaw; but to indulge them is to invite the gravest consequences."

Mrs. Walker said, "Well, that's for a parent to judge, Cousin Jane. The consequence in this case is that the Shaws are here—and I don't find that such a *grave* matter." She smiled. Susan melted inside. 'How could Daddy not be devastated by that smile?' she thought. Mrs. Walker hurried on before Cousin Jane could interrupt, "I hope you passed a restful night, Mr. Shaw."

"Oh, yes, absolutely, thank you. I slept like a log. Uncle S— I mean, Mr. Hollister put us both to sleep with an endless lecture on politics."

"Oh, Mr. Hollister!" she laughed. "He is a dreadful filibusterer, isn't he? He dabbles in land speculation, you know, and tried to get into local politics, and comes to grief in nearly everything, and then blames it all on the Republicans. One must be very firm with Mr. Hollister. I feel sorry for his poor wife."

"Most unsuitable neighbors," Cousin Jane said. "They are the vulgarest of the vulgar. Of course, the whole idea of moving here was a mistake, and I was opposed to it from the first. But naturally the late Mr. Walker would not listen to *me*. He was a stubborn and misguided man."

"You are speaking of my husband," Mrs. Walker said quietly.

"I apologize, Isabelle. I did not mean to single him out

for any special opprobrium. All men, after all, are stubborn and misguided—when they are not merely weak and misguided."

A pall of silence settled over them. Robert's face wore a look of stoic blankness; he sat like a ramrod, staring straight ahead, as though he were on parade. Victoria's expression was so miserable that Susan couldn't bear to look any more. She glanced about the room, half-seeing things which in happier circumstances would have delighted her: a white marble fireplace; a glass case containing—jewels?—no, stuffed hummingbirds; a massive mirror whose frame was decorated with gilt bunches of grapes and carved leaves; a vase full of peacock feathers . . .

"Mr. Shaw!" Cousin Jane said, so suddenly that they all jumped. "May I enquire as to your line of endeavor?"

"Ah—I beg your pardon?"

Cousin Jane closed her eyes. "What do you do in the city?"

"Oh! I'm with Dexler and Feldman. We make—"

"Papa is in finance," Susan plunged in, just in time to prevent him from saying "radio and television parts."

"That's right," he said, recovering from the near-fumble. "I take care of the, ah, financial end of the business." His face turned red.

"In-deed?" Cousin Jane said. She opened her eyes again and brought them to bear on Susan. "In *my* day, children never spoke until spoken to."

"Well," Susan muttered, "things are changing."

"They are indeed—and changing steadily for the worse. One's duty to maintain the highest standards becomes more burdensome every day."

There was another silence, which was broken at last by a relieved cry from Mrs. Walker:

"Ah! Here comes Maggie with the tea."

Mrs. Walker was looking over her shoulder. Following her gaze to a corner of the parlor, Susan noticed for the first time a tall doorway draped in green velvet portieres. She still had only a hazy notion of how the house was arranged, but it seemed to her that this doorway must open into the hall where the elevator was. A tinkling sound on the other side announced Maggie's approach. And here she was, a plump little woman maneuvering a tray past the velvet fringes. The tray was piled high with cups and saucers and the tea pot and silverware and napkins and sugar and cream and butter and rolls. Maggie's round freckled face was set in a frown of concentration. She advanced into the parlor step by step, her eyes fixed on the floor just ahead of her, the tip of her tongue thrust out between her tightened lips. Susan found that she was holding her breath. Everyone else seemed to be doing the same . . .

Ah! Maggie was going to succeed. She had reached the center of the room. Her tray hovered over the delicate cherrywood table by Mrs. Walker's side. She lifted her face with the beginnings of a triumphant smile on it, turned as if to receive everyone's congratulations— and caught sight of Mr. Shaw.

She gasped. Her face went white. "Mer-r-rciful hivvens!" she moaned. Her eyes turned up in their sockets. The tray fell from her hands, slithered over the edge of the table, and precipitated its load to the floor with a crash. There was a second crash as Maggie fell over backwards in a dead faint.

. . . happened again, and Cousin Jane
used it as an excuse to throw us out. We
took a walk because we didn't know what
else to do. I began to hope again that there
was still a chance, but when we got back
Cousin Jane smashed my hopes probably
forever . . .

They were all paralyzed for a moment with shock and surprise. Then Mrs. Walker jumped out of her chair. A fragment of porcelain crunched under her foot as she hurried around the wreckage to kneel by Maggie.

"Bobbie, quick! Fetch my smelling salts. I think they're in my reticule up in my room."

Robert dashed off, throwing one frightened glance back over his shoulder as he went. They heard his feet thundering up the stairs.

Victoria leaped up and ran over to her mother, who was now rubbing Maggie's wrists. Mrs. Walker waved her off, saying, "No, dear, I can manage for a moment. Bring a towel, will you? The tea is soaking into the rug." Victoria darted away, wringing her hands.

Cousin Jane closed her eyes and said, "Really, Isabelle, this is distressing. That chinaware was very costly, I believe. I remember Mr. Walker's Aunt Sophronia telling me that she had gone to a great deal of trouble to find that particular pattern."

Mr. Shaw half rose from his chair and asked, "Can I help in some way?"

"Oh, no, thank you, Mr. Shaw, I— Please remain

seated. I do hope you'll forgive us for this little—con-tretemps."

"This sort of thing," Cousin Jane pronounced, her eyes still closed, "does not occur in well-regulated house-holds."

Susan jumped out of her chair, knelt on the other side of Maggie, murmured, "Please let me help," and began to rub Maggie's free wrist.

Mrs. Walker said, "Thank you, Susan," and gave her a smile that made her glow with pleasure. But pain was mixed with her feelings, too, now that she was close enough to see how hollow Mrs. Walker's eyes looked, and how drawn her face was.

"Having an ill-trained servant is more trouble than having no servant at all," Cousin Jane said.

A flush came over Mrs. Walker's cheeks, and her mouth tightened; but before she could answer, Victoria and Robert came rushing back into the room. Victoria began to sop up the spilt tea and pile the broken china on the tray. Robert, with a shaking hand, thrust a tiny unstoppered vial under Maggie's nose.

"All right!" Mrs. Walker said, attempting a cheerful air. "We'll have her around in no time now," and she rubbed briskly away at Maggie's left wrist, while Susan, who had never done this before and was only imitating her, did the same on the right. "Maggie? Maggie? There's a dear!"

Maggie stirred, and her eyelids fluttered. "Oh, Mum," she muttered in a hoarse undertone, "am I still alive, then?"

"Of course you are, silly!"

Maggie's eyes opened. She looked at Mrs. Walker with a puzzled, apologetic expression. "Oh, I'm so sorry, Mum. I thought it was the last minute of me mortal life."

"What was it, Maggie? You frightened us all half to death!"

"Frightened, is it? Sure, Mum, I saw a sign that would make the very flesh of you melt away from your bones with fright."

Cousin Jane sniffed.

"Sit up, Maggie dear, it's all right now. How *could* you see any such thing right here in our own parlor?"

Maggie struggled into a sitting position. "Our own parlor or not, Mum, me second sight sees what it sees. I jist lifts me eyes from me tray and turns me head—" She demonstrated, with the result that she now saw Susan for the first time.

Her eyes widened with horror. She uttered a dying scream and fell backwards. Mrs. Walker seized her just in time to prevent her head from banging on the floor.

Susan dropped the wrist she had been rubbing, and fell back on her heels in bewilderment. Mrs. Walker cried, "Maggie! What *is* the matter?" Robert began to wave the smelling salts again. Victoria scurried across the floor on her hands and knees and began to rub Maggie's cheeks. Mr. Shaw jumped up, stepping on his hat and crushing it, and cried, "Let's get her into a chair!"

Cousin Jane was the only one who was paying no attention to Maggie. Her eyes were fastened on Mr. Shaw, and they glittered with suspicion.

"Mr. Shaw!" she said like the crack of a whip. Everyone fell silent and turned to look at her. "This is a most peculiar circumstance, is it not?"

"It certainly is! I never saw anything like—"

"Perhaps you are prepared to offer some explanation."

"Who, me?" Mr. Shaw cried. "I have no more idea—"

"Were you acquainted with this unfortunate woman?"

74

"No! I never saw her before in my life."

"In-deed? I had the distinct impression that she was made insensible by the shock of seeing and recognizing you. I was going to overlook that impression. However, the sight of your daughter has had the same unhappy effect on her. The coincidence seems to me too pointed to be ignored. It was my hope that you could enlighten me."

The coincidence was not only pointed, it was dumbfounding. Mr. Shaw and Susan gaped at Cousin Jane, and at Maggie, and at each other. "I—I don't know what to say," Mr. Shaw finally stammered.

Cousin Jane compressed her lips and turned to Mrs. Walker. "Isabelle, in view of the fact that Mr. Shaw and Miss Shaw have such an unsettling effect on Maggie, do you not think it would be wise if they were elsewhere when she comes to?"

Mrs. Walker flushed, and raised her eyes to Mr. Shaw with an agonized look.

"Mrs. Walker," he said, "I'm sorry. I really am. I don't know why we have such an effect on Maggie, but since we do, we had better go. Thank you for your hospitality, and . . ."

"Oh, Mr. Shaw, I—I am devastated." Mrs. Walker made a helpless little gesture. "I'm sorrier than I can say that things have— Let us hope that we can meet again under happier circumstances."

Cousin Jane stood, and stared at Susan while she scrambled to her feet and joined her father. Then she advanced on them, making them fall back toward the door. Everyone was murmuring "Goodbye, goodbye." Susan and Robert and Victoria exchanged despairing looks. "Good day, good day, most regrettable," Cousin Jane said. A gleam of malice shone briefly behind her glasses as she held the door for the Shaws. It closed after them with a thump.

Stunned, they walked down the path to Ward Lane. There Mr. Shaw suddenly hurled his ruined hat into the dust and kicked it. "Good *night!*" he ground out through his teeth. "What a poisonous woman!"

Susan looked back at the house where her hopes lay in shambles, and choked down her tears.

There seemed to be no point in going back to the Hollisters' merely to sit around. They began to trudge down the lane.

"Well," Mr. Shaw said after a while, "looks like we're not going to get to the elevator until tonight. But tonight is *it*. We're going to stay up and watch until it's safe to go, and go."

"All right," she said dully.

"Listen, what *was* that business with Maggie, anyway?"

"I don't know. Maybe we look like somebody else that she—I don't know."

"Somebody else who scares the living daylights out of her, then. Was anybody threatening her or anything?"

"No . . . Oh! Vicky did say that she's been talking

about 'signs' or something like that. She's awfully super-stitious. Maybe we look like somebody she used to know who died, and she thinks we're ghosts."

"Hmm . . . Wish we could throw that kind of scare into that cousin of theirs! Poor Isabelle!"

"Oh, Daddy!" she said, turning to him with desperate appeal. "Isn't it awful? We can't go away without doing *some*thing to help her out."

"Right!" he said, nodding his head. "Absolutely right."

Her heart leaped up. "Oh, Daddy, it would just solve everything if you—"

"Come on, Susie," he broke in with a short laugh. "Will you just drop that idea, please? I'm sure we can help her out and still go back to the twentieth century. Let me think a bit . . ."

But hope, that tiny, stubborn flame, was alight in her heart once more. There was still the rest of the day left . . . And he had called her by name—not "poor Mrs. Walker," but "poor Isabelle!" Surely that meant something; some change of attitude that he might not even be aware of himself yet. And she, Mrs. Walker, had *actually said*, "I hope we meet again under happier cir-cumstances." Well, there was still the rest of the day to get them together again somehow. She and Victoria and Robert would have to have a council of war as soon as possible. The main problem now was how to get around Cousin Jane . . . She shivered. No wonder the Walkers had shown such gloom at the mere mention of her name! But still, dragon though she was, she couldn't be everywhere at once, could she . . . ?

Thus preoccupied with their thoughts, they walked almost as far as the stream where they had napped yesterday morning, then turned around and went back.

Mrs. Hollister met them at the door. She murmured,

"Oh, Mr. Shaw," and began to writhe.

"What's the matter?"

"It's," Mrs. Hollister gasped. "I mean—she's—" She signalled toward the parlor with her eyes, twisted her hands, and fled to the shelter of the kitchen.

"Mr. Shaw!" snapped a familiar voice.

There, in the doorway of the parlor, bonneted and clasping a tightly-furled black umbrella, stood Cousin Jane.

Mr. Shaw's nostrils turned white. "Ah," he said in a stiff voice.

"My business is brief," Cousin Jane said. Her eyes glittered at them. "I shall detain you no more than a minute. Mrs. Walker's servant has revived, and I have been questioning her very closely."

She paused to see what effect this announcement had on them, and seemed disappointed that it had none. She continued:

"I do not know what to make of her story. One must consider that she is ignorant and filled with superstitions; on the other hand, her sincerity is beyond question. She claims she fainted because she believed you to be supernatural figures, a 'sign' or some such rubbish —apparently she is given to hysterical notions of that sort. But I cannot lightly dismiss her reasons for so believing. She has an unshakable conviction that at midnight of the night before last, she saw the two of you, surrounded by a ghostly glow—in the hallway of the Walkers' house."

Susan hoped that she was successful in suppressing her gasp. *That* was it! She stared hard at a highlight flashing from one lens of Cousin Jane's pince-nez, and tried to keep her face expressionless.

"Ridiculous!" Mr. Shaw said in a convincing tone.

"Indeed?" Cousin Jane sniffed. "Perhaps. It is not for me to say without further evidence whether the woman's 'vision' was the product of her feverish imagination, or of something more, shall we say, *substantial.*"

Cousin Jane paused, and compressed her lips.

"Now look here!" Mr. Shaw said. "Are you implying something?"

"I imply nothing, Mr. Shaw, that a clear conscience would find offensive. Let me continue. I discovered almost as soon as I arrived this morning that you and your daughter had succeeded within a *very* short space of time in exerting a peculiar influence over Robert and Victoria. I discovered that you had exerted that influence in order to scrape an acquaintance with their mother. Now I have just discovered from Mrs. Hollister that you came here, and are staying here, *without baggage.* You travel light, Mr. Shaw—for a person 'in finance.' One cannot help wondering what kind of 'finance' you actually deal in."

Mr. Shaw clenched his fists and said, "What are you getting at?"

"Very well, Mr. Shaw, I will not mince words with you. I find everything about you irregular—highly irregular. I have no option under the circumstances but to forbid you to see or speak to my kinswoman, Mrs. Walker, any further. As for you, Miss Shaw, I forbid you to have any further connection whatsoever with Robert or Victoria."

Mr. Shaw took two steps forward, and said, "Who the devil are *you* to go around saying who we can or can't see?"

"I believe you to be a thoroughgoing scoundrel, sir! I warn you that if you give me the slightest pretext, I shall report you to the nearest police station!"

"You can report me wherever and whenever you like.

And if it's a pretext you're waiting for"—Mr. Shaw snapped his fingers an inch from Cousin Jane's nose— "I hope that will serve!"

She fell back a step. Her face went crimson, and her pince-nez dropped off her nose. Half raising her umbrella, she said in a voice that shook with fury, "Do not press me too far, my man! I have said what I came to say, and I am now leaving. Stand aside!"

"Go around, blast you!" he roared.

They stood their ground for perhaps a quarter of a minute, glaring at each other. Then Cousin Jane stabbed the tip of her umbrella into the floor, and, uttering little huffs and groans of rage, walked around Mr. Shaw and stamped out of the house.

⊰ 10. SUSAN AT THE END OF HER ROPE ⊱

> . . . no more hope for getting Daddy and
> Mrs. Walker together, as far as I could see.
> Daddy didn't seem to mind so much but I
> was sick. He meant it about helping her,
> though. He had figured out a plan while we
> were walking. We started to carry it out and
> ran smack into another disaster . . .

"By George!" Mr. Shaw gasped. He wiped his forehead with his handkerchief. His face was white, and his hands shook. "Whew! Boy oh boy, how I'd love to—!" He clenched his teeth and rubbed his hands together as though demolishing a noxious insect. "Hey, chick, what's the matter? Come on, it's all right; it's all over now."

"We won't—we won't get to see—Mrs. Walker—again—will we?" she wept.

"Anh-h-h! I've got half a mind to go over there right now just to show that flaming rhinoceros that she can't forbid *me* anything! If I didn't think she'd make even more trouble for poor Isabelle, I'd—oh lord, I don't know what! We *have* to get the Walkers out from under before we go—and I think I know how to do it."

He led her over to a moth-eaten purple plush sofa, and they sat down.

"It's nothing new," she went on. "It's just a way to get Isa—Mrs. Walker to accept the treasure. When you were telling me about your adventures here, didn't you mention a lawyer who was handling Mrs. Walker's investments?"

"Mr. Branscomb," she said in a dull voice.

"That was it—Branscomb. Wait here a sec—I have to talk to Mrs. H."

His voice and Mrs. Hollister's murmur sounded for a while in the kitchen. Then he was back.

"All right. She doesn't know his address, but he's in town and I'll find him. What we'll do is put the money in a bank under Branscomb's charge. He can tell Mrs. Walker that she hasn't lost everything, as they previously thought—one or two of her investments are rallying again. It's as simple as that. And of course, when she's on her feet again, she can send Cousin Jane back to wherever she came from.

"Now, Mrs. H. says there's a farmer named Knutsen near here who can give us a ride, so I'm going to go and arrange for one. While I'm doing that, you get a sack from the stable and bring back as much gold as you can carry by yourself. Whatever you can bring we'll take into town in Knutsen's buggy, and use it to set up the bank account. We can bring a trunk or chest back with us, and tonight before we leave we'll put the rest of the money in it. Branscomb will have instructions to pick it up here tomorrow and deposit it. Okay?"

"Okay . . ."

"Honey, I'm sorry, but it's really all I can do."

"I know."

They went out on the veranda.

"All right, chick. I'll see you here in a while. Just bring back what you can carry without a struggle." He squeezed her shoulders, kissed her on the forehead, and set off.

She lurked along the hedge for a while, waiting to see if Victoria or Robert would manage to slip out. She was going to have to tell them that their plan had failed. She was going to have to say goodbye forever, unless they could think of some desperate last-minute plan to—what, what, what? Her vision blurred with tears.

Victoria and Robert did not come out.

She sighed, and went into the Hollisters' stable. There was a pile of sacks draped over the frame of the grindstone. She picked one, folded it, and trudged out to the road.

It was another one of those beautiful days: bright blue sky with pillowy clouds, a mild sweet-smelling breeze, birds everywhere, butterflies wavering from flower to flower. She looked at it with anguish in her heart. Goodbye flowers, goodbye fields and woods and singing birds . . . Oh, if her father would just— A feeling of intense anger suddenly welled up inside her. He was so blind, so stupid, so stick-in-the-mud! Couldn't even see the fantastic gift that was being laid at his feet! Didn't *want* to see it!

She was still muttering to herself when she came to the forked stick, although part of her mind was trying to tell her that it really wasn't his fault. If nothing happened when he looked at Mrs. Walker—well, nothing happened. And that was that.

She sighed, looked up and down the road to make sure it was clear, and crawled into the thicket.

A burning, copper-tasting sensation clamped down on her tougue. Yesterday she had left dead leaves spread over the sackful of treasure. Now the leaves were all pushed aside, and there was nothing before her eyes but the tunnel's bare earth floor.

⊰⊱ ⊰⊱ ⊰⊱ ⊰⊱ ⊰⊱ ⊰⊱

When the sick dizzy feeling cleared from her head, she realized that of course it must have been Robert and Victoria. Robert had been worried about the treasure's safety. They had probably moved it last evening, intending to tell her this morning; and then had forgotten, in the shock of Cousin Jane's unexpected arrival.

She trotted back, trying to ignore the pain in her ankle. Good grief, this complicated the situation . . . ! She would have to see them somehow, Cousin Jane or no Cousin Jane, and find out where they'd put it, so that her father could—

But how to do it? Disheveled and panting, she stood by the Walkers' front gate and stared at the house. She couldn't just wait around for them to come out . . .

"Meow!" Toby said in the hedge.

She looked. A hand appeared over the top of the

foliage, beckoned, and vanished.

Ah! She hurried around through the Hollisters' gate. Robert and Victoria were huddled under the hedge.

"Sue!" Robert whispered before she could say anything. "Cousin Jane doesn't know we've escaped yet—I hope! We're not allowed to see you any more. We're not even allowed out of the house. We have to set up a communication post somewhere, quick."

"She's made us start to pack up our clothes and belongings, Sue!" Victoria said. "We only managed to slip away because she's in Mama's room. Oh, I hate her!— I don't care if it *is* wicked, I hate her! She's picking out all the furniture to be auctioned off, and poor Mama—"

"*Listen,*" Susan broke in, "where is it?"

"Where's what?" Robert asked.

"The treasure, the treasure!" she almost shouted. "Where did you put the treasure?"

Their silence and their puzzled eyes told her that the unimaginable worst had happened.

"Oh," she moaned.

"What's the matter, Sue?" Victoria whispered.

"It's gone," she choked. "It's *gone!*" She collapsed with her head in her arms, sobbing. They patted her back and murmured.

"I ought to be drummed out of the regiment!" Robert muttered after a while. "It's my fault—I knew it wasn't safe out there, but I didn't do anything about it."

"But how could anyone find it?" Victoria said in a cracked voice. "Who would *ever* look in a place like that?"

Robert sighed. "Well, boys would, for one—if they were bird's-nesting. Or a tramp's dog . . . Oh, thunderation! I can't bear it when you cry, Sue, please stop."

"It's not just the treasure," she wept. "It's everything.

Our whole plan's a failure. Daddy *won't* fall in love with your Mama and he—he insists on going—back tonight, and it's all over!"

At last Robert said in a faraway voice, "Don't feel bad, Sue. I think we've kind of known since yesterday afternoon that it was going to be a frost. Mama . . . I don't know, she—"

"Her heart," Victoria gulped, "also remains—untouched. Oh, I can't understand it!" She began to cry too.

"I feel like I'm leaving you in the lur-ur-urch!" Susan wept.

"Don't feel that way, Sue," Victoria sobbed. "You did everything you could."

"It's really totus dexter, Sue," Robert murmured. "I mean, we're just where we were anyway before you came along. In fact, we're better off, because if you hadn't chased Mr. Sweeney away—"

"Oh!" Victoria gasped. She straightened up and wiped her eyes with the back of her hand. "*Oh!* Before you came along—! Sue! Before you came along, I went to a wishing well, and I wished—and I got my wish! *Why wouldn't it work again?*"

"But the witch is in the twentieth century," Susan said hopelessly, "and we're all here."

"Oh, pooh! What difference does that make? She's a witch, she can do what she wants. Oh! Bobbie! Let's both sacrifice somthing this time and *double* the power of the wish!"

"Hey, that's a capital idea, Vick!" Robert said. "There's a strategic problem, though—we have to do it so Cousin Jane doesn't know we're doing it."

"Oh, mercy, that's right . . . ! I know—you go back and fetch the sacrifices, Bobbie. You're the expert forager, you'd have a better chance of getting past Cousin

85

Jane than I would. I'll go to the stable and watch your back bedroom window. You can drop the things out the window into the bushes. Then even if Cousin Jane catches you, I can still get the things and make a run for the well by myself."

"That's it—divided forces! Gosh, Vick, you'd make a great general—if they allowed girls in the Army."

"Pooh! Girls are too sensible to *want* to be in the Army. Now! We have to decide what we're going to sacrifice. Remember, it has to be something you really love, or it won't have any effect."

Robert considered. He frowned, bit his lip, looked away from his sister, looked back, and slowly stiffened his spine. "Very well, I'll—" He faltered an instant, then went on with a rush. "I'll give my arrowhead collection."

"Oh, Bobbie, that's noble! I'm going to give my little silver mirror that Mama gave me."

"That belonged to Great-great-great-grandmother Wayne," Robert whispered. "Back in the *Revolution*."

"I know," Victoria sighed. "But this is more important than—"

"Wait!" Susan said. "Don't—" She was going to say, "Don't throw away your treasures for nothing," but Victoria stopped her by gently laying her finger against Susan's lips. Perhaps she could see that Susan was at the end of hope. "Ssssh!" she whispered. "Don't say anything. Remember, it's always darkest before dawn."

"It's our campaign now, Sue." Robert added. "You did everything you could. Now it's up to us." He squeezed her hand. "Nil desperandum! We'll see you again when we can. Let's go, Vick!"

"Goodbye, Sue. Don't worry—*please.*—How are you going to get back into the house, Bobbie?"

"I think that window is still open in the sun parlor."

They crawled away along the hedge, talking in low tones, and vanished into the neglected tangle of shrubbery at the back of the Hollister property.

Susan watched them out of sight. Her heart felt like a chunk of iron. She was convinced that this was the last she would ever see of them. And she had been so numb that she hadn't even said goodbye . . .

The Shaws waited in their rooms for night to come.

Mr. Shaw, not wanting to hear any more about Republican villainy from Mr. Hollister, told Mrs. Hollister that he was feeling unwell, and asked for a light supper that could be sent upstairs on a tray. As a matter of fact, he was feeling unwell. The loss of the treasure, and hence his inability to help Mrs. Walker, had thrown him into a depression. When the tray came up neither he nor Susan could look at it.

Time oozed on. They endured as best they could. Mr. Shaw leafed through a stack of newspapers. Susan tried to write a goodbye letter to Victoria and Robert. After many false starts and long periods of staring into space, she produced a note that said, "Dear Vicky and Bobbie: Goodbye. I have to go back. I'm sorry our plans failed. I don't think I will ever be happy again. Love, Susan."

She thought she had run out of tears, but she hadn't.

Her father came up behind her quietly and put his hands on her shoulders. "Try to look at it this way, Susie," he pleaded. "This all happened a long time ago, really. It just *seems* to be happening now. But we're really twentieth-century people, honey. All this—" he waved a hand to include the fields and woods, and the nearby town, and the Hollister and Walker houses, and their inhabitants "—all this is *gone*. It was all over and done with before we were even born."

She knew, in a sense, he was right, but she could not be convinced. He didn't sound fully convinced himself.

Mr. Hollister came home and brayed at his wife. She murmured back. The catbird that Susan had heard when she first arrived in the nineteenth century sang, and scolded *mew, mew,* and sang again. A golden evening declined into dusk. Mrs. Hollister brought candles up, and took away their untouched food.

To help pass the time, Susan brought her diary up to date. She wrote at the end of her last entry:

> *. . . afraid that the idea wouldn't work. I just had a feeling that something like that doesn't happen twice. Or maybe Vicky and Bobbie never got to the well. Anyway, nothing has happened. Nothing is going to happen. There isn't enough time left to change anything now. We're going back to the twentieth century and I am absolutely in despair.*

⋐ 11. LADY IN DISTRESS ⋑

"Hey!" Charles said. "Is that the end of it?"

After the word "despair" in Susan's diary there was more than half a page, all blank. The facing page was blank. I searched through the rest of the pages to the back cover. They were all blank.

"Oh, no," I groaned.

"But the Shaws *didn't* come back to the twentieth century, did they?" Charles asked.

"No! I'm positive they didn't—I would've heard about it, I would've seen them around the apartment building. And listen, there's that old photograph—they're all in it, Shaws and Walkers both!"

He got that look on his face again. "Edward, the fact is that you never saw Mrs. Walker, and you never saw Victoria, and you never saw Robert. For that matter, how well did you actually know the Shaws?"

"Oh—slightly."

"Slightly . . . Besides which, it's a very grainy photograph. I wonder if you haven't jumped to some mistaken conclusions. The people in that photograph may have nothing to do with the people in this—this story of yours."

"*Story!* Blast it, Charles, didn't I tell you about Susan before we read the diary? And wasn't everything in the diary absolutely consistent with what I told you? Story! It's *real*, man!"

"Mmmm . . ."

"And another thing: I'm the only person in the world except Mrs. Clutchett who could have any notion of what this diary is about. And it falls into my hands *because someone calls me up to tell me where it is.* How do you explain *that?*"

"Well . . . I don't. But there must be some simple answer. Hey, calm down! It can't be worth getting so excited about."

"What d'you mean, calm down? It's *maddening* not to be able to know what happened!"

"Let me take you to lunch," he suggested soothingly.

"No, thanks. I'm not hungry."

At the front door he said, "Listen, if anything else turns up about this business, keep me posted, will you?"

"Why should I keep *you* posted, you skeptic?"

"Oh, I'm a skeptic, all right; as an historian I have to be. But it's never prevented me from enjoying a good yarn."

A good yarn, forsooth! There are times when I could kick Charles with the greatest of pleasure. That superior, comomn-sensical air of his! I was being unfair, I suppose. But it irked me beyond endurance to be confronted with this mystery. Here was the diary, ending in the Shaws' total defeat. Here was the photograph, showing the Shaws and Walkers triumphant. How had they ever managed to overcome all the obstacles in their way?

Or—I kept pushing away the dreadful thought, and it kept coming back—or *had* they? Was Charles perhaps right about the photograph? *Was* it just wishful thinking and self-delusion on my part to see Susan and Mr. Shaw and Mrs. Shaw and Robert and Victoria in those grainy, time-darkened, nineteenth-century faces . . . ?

Oh, blast Charles, anyway!

I looked up, and saw that I was one block from home, and that a crowd was collecting on the sidewalks of Ward Street.

And good reason for it, too! Despondent as I was, I felt my heart lifting at the sight before me. There was the most gorgeous old-fashioned automobile standing by the curb. It was taller than I am, and nearly as long as a fire engine, and only the back part was enclosed; the chauffeur's seat was open to the weather. Its condition was perfect. It was blue, so dark as to look almost black, and polished like glass. Silver trim dazzled in the sun, and there were varnished wooden spokes in the wheels.

I pushed through the crowd to get a closer look, and suddenly the chauffeur had me by the arm. He was a swarthy individual in a uniform of impeccable black, including polished black leather puttees. He murmured to me in a lisping foreign accent:

"Yes, sir, very opportune, sir, I beg your pardon, but as you see, a slight mishap, sir, the lady requests your assistance, sir."

The right front tire was flat.

"You mean—?" I began.

"Yes, sir, a trifling matter, sir, she will be most grateful, I have the tools all ready, sir."

I hesitated. I wanted to go home and think, and I am not very mechanically inclined anyway, and there were plenty of other men in the crowd who looked more competent than I; and besides, I had always thought that such matters were the chauffeur's job.

"If you will be so kind, sir, the lady is most anguished, sir."

I saw a tiny fragile white-haired woman in the enclosed part of the car. She was wearing jewels and silvery furs (furs! in August!) and her withered face did have an air of vague, I could almost say absentminded, distress.

"Oh, all right," I said—I'm afraid with ill grace.

The chauffeur murmured, "Yes, sir, much obliged, sir, here is the jack, sir," and I knelt down to a half-hour of frustrating labor and sweat. Everything went contrariwise. The chauffeur hovered over me, murmuring in an encouraging tone, but refusing to touch anything himself. Men in the crowd made comments and suggestions, but whenever someone stepped forward to give me a hand he would be politely turned back by the murmuring chauffeur. I really don't know how I succeeded in figuring out the jack, and wrenching off the nuts, and extricating the spare wheel from its well in the front fender, and getting the job done. But I did, and then stood up, dripping and grease-stained and in a savage humor.

"Thank you, sir, well done, sir, the lady would like to express her gratitude, sir."

She had pulled a little folding walnut writing desk from its compartment behind the chauffeur's seat, and was writing with—so help me!—a goose-quill pen. 'Is she making out a check?' I wondered. Whatever it was, she put it in an envelope; and the chauffeur, cranking down the window between his seat and the rear compartment, took the envelope from her skinny claws, and handed it over to me.

Then he saluted, leaped into his seat, started up the motor with an incredible blast of noise that made the whole crowd jump; and that vast, stately automobile darted away through the traffic with all the agility of a sports car.

"Boy, they better get that muffler fixed," one of the bystanders said. I agreed, with my ears ringing.

The envelope was made of beautiful thick creamy paper. My fingers had smudged it with grease already; and although I was twitching with curiosity to see what was inside, I decided that I could wait until I had washed up. I was only a block away from home.

There was a new message on the back wall of the elevator. It was written in black crayon, and it said, "Bodoni couldn't fix a roller skate."

Poor Mr. Bodoni! He had been getting a lot of insults like that lately. The elevator, which had been slow and noisy before the Shaws disappeared in it, had steadily gotten slower and noisier ever since. Frequently these days it lurched from side to side in the shaft and came to a shuddering near-halt between floors. I think perhaps its travels through time had put too much strain on the mechanism. The increasingly nervous tenants showered Mr. Bodoni with complaints. He could be seen nearly every day poking around in the works with wrench, oil can, and responsible frown—but to no avail. One day someone wrote in red chalk on the back wall of the elevator, "Is this an elevator or a hearse?" The idea caught on, and similar messages began to appear as fast as Mr. Bodoni could scrub them off: "Greased Lightning," "Please replace squirrel in motor," "I'm too young to die!" and so forth.

Nowadays when Mr. Bodoni even suspected that you were going to complain about the elevator, he would back away with a hunted look in his eye, waving his hands and saying, "Not dangerous! Don't you believe! A little slow, maybe, but not dangerous, don't worry!" I guess I am the only tenant who didn't complain; knowing, as the others couldn't, what the elevator had been through.

But I felt like complaining now. It was taking forever

to get to the fifth floor where I live, and my impatience to see what was in the envelope was growing. "Come *on,* old horse," I muttered, patting its flank. It responded by giving another earthquake-lurch and a groan, and slowing down.

Eventually the arrow shuddered to a stop on 5, and the door sighed and rumbled open. I dashed to my apartment and scrubbed my hands at the kitchen sink. The grease was as stubborn as a second skin, and in the end I just wiped off what was left on the dish-towel. Now at last I could open the envelope.

It was not a check inside, but a note on the same kind of thick beautiful paper as the envelope was made of. All it said, in tiny wavery spider-web-thin letters, was:

> *Reservations for this year are filled,*
> *but you may send a message. I suggest*
> *a Special Notice.*

I sat down.

Nothing today was making much sense . . .

For the next hour I puzzled over it all without reaching any conclusions, except the very tentative one that the lady who had phoned me was the same person I had seen in the automobile. All I had to go on was the fact that the automobile's roar had sounded like the noise on the phone; and the fact, or impression, that the handwriting on the note *looked* the way the voice on the phone had *sounded,* if you see what I mean. Pretty thin evidence, I admit . . . But wait, there was another similarity. They both—or she, if it was the same person—had singled me out. The voice on the phone had definitely mentioned my number, and the chauffeur had seized my arm as though he had been instructed to wait for help until I came along. Well, all right—but what did it mean? Had I been called because I was the only person who could know what Susan's diary was about? Maybe. But surely I hadn't been picked by the chauffeur because I was the only person who could change that wheel . . . As for the note, which I now read for the twentieth time—my mind knocked against it with all the effect of a moth trying to go through a windowpane.

There was a rap on my door.

It was Mr. Bodoni, his face shining with perspiration and his arms laden with newspapers. He collected these from the tenants to sell; there was an enormous stack in the basement.

"Gotny noospapers?" he said around his dead cigar.

"Nope," I sighed. I had given up telling him that I don't subscribe to a paper and rarely buy one.

"Yeah. Okay," he said. He shifted the bundle in his arms, and said, "Hot, hah?" and turned to go. Two words leaped out at me from the densely printed grey page on top of his load.

"Wait, hold it!" I cried. He turned back. "Can I have that page?"

"Hah?"

"That page there on top. Can I have it?"

"Yeah," he said, staring at me with puzzlement.

It was half a page, actually—the lower part. I tore it off, and thanked him, and closed the door.

Did you know—I never did until that moment—that the want ads in the newspaper begin with Legal Notices and continue with Special Notices?

Special Notices . . . I stood there, swallowing hard, and reading as fast as I could.

Blood plasma donors wanted . . .

I will not be responsible for debts incurred by anyone other than myself. Three of these, signed respectively by—well, no matter.

We have room to accept the dumping of approx. 3000 yds. of fill dirt . . .

NOTICE OF LIQUIDATION . . .

Oh, my word!

REWARD for info. leading to contact with Jane Hildegarde Clamp. Call TEM-8118.

Jane Hildegarde Clamp? *Jane Clamp?* Of course there could be no connection, but—

I reached for my phone and dialed. A professional, airline-stewardess kind of voice crooned, "Good afternoon, Tri-City Guaranty and Trust Company, may I help you?"

"Ah—" I said. I hadn't been expecting that. I don't know what I had been expecting. "I'm calling, ah, about that Personal Notice in the paper—"

"Just one moment, sir, I'll connect you with Mr. Thornley."

Some bloops and beeps and *sotto voce* mumbling, and then another professional, deep, money kind of voice said, "Thornley here."

"I'm calling about Jane Hildegarde Clamp."

"Ah! You have some information?"

"No, I want some. Can you tell me what this is all about?"

A slight pause, and then, "I'm sorry, sir, but the matter is confidential. I'm sure you'll understand."

"Can't you tell me anything? Is it Miss Clamp or Mrs. Clamp?"

"I'm sorry, sir, the matter is confidential. May I ask you why you called?"

"Well, the name seemed—I just heard of a name like it this morning."

"I see. Well, there are other names like it in the city.

We are *not* referring to—just a moment, please." Sounds of papers rustling. "We don't want to hear about Mrs. June Hilda Clamp of 2637 Larch Street, or Miss Joan H. Clamp of 1178 West 97th Street, or J. Helga Clamp of 21219 New Zealand Avenue. I might also say, although I'm sure I needn't warn *you*, sir, that we can make it uncomfortable for crank callers if we catch them. What we want is bona fide information about the whereabouts of Jane Hildegarde Clamp. We want to get in touch with her."

"I see . . . Well, thank you."

"Thank *you*, sir."

Well, so much for that. Another coincidence, no doubt. And yet . . . and yet I had the nagging suspicion that everything was pointing in some particular direction, and that I could make sense of it if only—if only—

But I couldn't make sense of it. I spent the rest of the day alternately trying and giving up, drinking coffee, pacing about, cooking dinner, going to a disappointing movie . . .

Late that evening I sat down with a sigh to read Susan's diary again. It had occurred to me that perhaps I had overlooked something in it that might give me a clue. I was right. As I neared the end of it, and again read that scene where a despairing Susan crouches under the hedge with Robert and Victoria, and Victoria proposes one last measure to save their plan from total ruin, and Susan says that even that measure is hopeless, because here they are in the nineteenth century whereas the witch is in the twentieth—as I read that for the second time my heart began to thud, and the hair on the back of my neck prickled.

That wavery voice on the telephone! That ancient creature in the huge automobile! Eureka!

⊰{ 12. THE ELEVATOR'S LAST TRIP }⊱

Of course I hadn't recognized the witch.

How could I? Whenever I thought of her at all, it was as Susan had described her: an eccentric, garish old woman with an umbrella, a newspaper, a sack of potatoes, and a vague manner, who was driven about on a motorcycle. Whereas *my* lady in distress— Well, no matter. She had changed her appearance and her mode of transportation, but the old vagueness was still there, and her way of doing things was the same. You helped her out, and she gave you something. But what she gave you was a mystery, a hint, a possibility. From there on, you had to figure out her meaning for yourself.

Well, now that I knew who she was, everything clicked into place in my mind. She *was* going to answer the Walker children's plea; and because I was the only person in the world who knew—and accepted—where the Shaws had gone, she had chosen me to carry out her plans.

The first phrase of her note was so roundabout that it took me a while to interpret, but I finally guessed it to mean that I could not go back to 1881 myself. The rest was straightforward enough. I could send a message to the Shaws. The means of sending it would have to be the elevator. The message itself would be the Special Notice.

But wait—I'd better be careful about that. Just because I'd found a Special Notice with a familiar name didn't mean that it was the one to go. I took the elevator down to the basement, and spent an hour rummaging through Mr. Bodoni's heap of newspapers. There were some pretty odd Special Notices to be found, but none that seemed closer to the purpose than the one I already had. That one, by the way, appeared in every paper I looked at. Tri-City Guaranty and Trust Company had been seeking contact with Jane Hildegarde Clamp for as far back as I could check. Curious . . .

Back in my apartment, I figured out what my strategy should be. If the Shaws did find the message in the elevator, they would be there for only one reason: to return to the twentieth century. But if they came back to the twentieth century, thereby using up their last trip on the elevator, the message might be useless. Therefore, they must be persuaded to read it before they took the irrevocable step.

I found a large manila mailing envelope and wrote on it with black crayon: SUSAN SHAW—MR. SHAW— DON'T COME DOWN UNTIL YOU READ WHAT'S INSIDE! Then I circled the Special Notice about Jane Hildegarde Clamp, to call the Shaws' attention to it; and put a question mark beside it to show that its significance was just a guess on my part. For a while I tried to think what it might mean to them, to figure out how it could possibly turn the tide of events where they were. But it was useless. With a sigh, I folded the sheet of newspaper and inserted it in the envelope, and went out in the hall to call the elevator.

The latest wisecrack about Mr. Bodoni's mechanical ability had been imperfectly scrubbed off, I noticed. I stuck the envelope to the rear wall with tape, and stepped back to view the effect. My message was as conspicuous as I could hope to make it. "Okay, old horse, do your stuff," I murmured to the elevator. It sighed, and the door trundled shut.

Well, it was out of my hands now. I went to bed. But doubts flooded over me, and I couldn't sleep. Had I done the right thing? How would I ever know? After an hour of tossing, I put on my bathrobe and rushed out to check the elevator. My message was gone. My heart lifted—and sank again. What did that prove, after all? Only that it was gone; perhaps to 1881, perhaps (just as likely) to the apartment of some nosy and not too scrupulous tenant . . .

How would I ever know . . . ?

⊰⟨ ⊰⟨ ⊰⟨ ⟩⊱ ⟩⊱ ⟩⊱

Saturday night was another sleepless one for me. At about nine-thirty Sunday morning I decided to go to the park; I thought that perhaps in the shade of a tree I might find some relief from the heat and from the questions that were still plaguing me. I pressed the elevator button and waited . . . And pressed again and waited. And waited.

Finally I took the stairs down. I ran into Mr. Bodoni at the front door. He was prepared for a Sunday outing too, in a black suit that made him look like a mourner at a gangster's funeral, and a straw hat, and a new (but of course unlit) cigar.

"Hey, Mr. Bodoni, what's the matter with the elevator?" I asked.

"Busted," he said with a huge smile. "Busted for good. Finished. I call the owners, they gonna replace. All brand-new parts—everyting!" No more gestures of apology: Mr. Bodoni was a free man.

"Oh," I said.

100

"Whatsa matter, you crazy or someting, you don't wanna new one?"

"Well . . . I was kind of attached to the old beast. How did it go?"

"Hah?"

"How did it bust?"

"Boy oh boy!" he said, beginning to frown. "Some business! I don't even wanna tink about!" His voice dropped to a confidential murmur. "You wanna know someting? Crazy lady in there!"

"What?"

"Yeah! Boy oh boy, I don't even wanna talk about!"

Nevertheless, I didn't have to prompt him to tell me the whole story.

In order to escape the heat late last night, he had gone down into the basement, where it was five degrees cooler than anywhere else. Settled in a camp chair, in his undershirt, a can of cold beer within reach, the early edition of the Sunday papers in his lap opened to the comics section, he slipped into a state of perfect contentment.

It lasted perhaps fifteen minutes.

A faint rhythmic banging began to intrude on his consciousness. It seemed to be coming from—from the elevator shaft . . . Oh oh! Had the elevator broken down at last? Was somebody stuck? He looked up at the arrow. No, it was moving; moving to the left. The banging became louder. It sounded as if someone were trying to do grievous damage. Indignation welled up in Mr. Bodoni's heart; he had no love for the elevator, but it was his responsibility. They shouldn't do that! Thunderous blows drowned out the sigh of the opening door. Mr. Bodoni stood up, prepared to defend his elevator against carousing delinquents or perhaps some tenant who had had too much to drink. "Hey!" he cried, taking one step forward, only to be stopped dead in his tracks by the most ferocious glare he had ever encountered.

It was not coming from a juvenile hoodlum or a drunk, but from a woman. She was awkwardly seated, as one entirely unaccustomed to such a position, on the floor of the elevator. Her stout figure was dressed in a red flannel robe. Her face, under a ruffled cap, was purple with rage, and her eyes glittered behind pince-nez glasses. The black umbrella with which she had been battering the elevator door was raised to strike another blow.

Mr. Bodoni managed another, and much more feeble, "Hey."

"I'll hey you, my man!" the woman shouted in a voice that was even more piercing than her eyes. "Who are you? What is the meaning of this outrage?"

"Outrage" had been a familiar word of late. Mr. Bodoni's wits rallied. "Not dangerous," he said, waving conciliatory hands. "A little slow maybe, yeah, but not dangerous. Don't hit, the paint job won't take it."

"Stop talking rubbish!" she shouted. "I demand an explanation!"

"No rubbish," Mr. Bodoni protested. "It's a little old, is all. Loose parts."

"I won't have any *more* of this lunatic raving!" she cried. "I am in severe pain. I require medical attention. Above all, I wish to return. And *you* stand there—!"

"Madame," a man's voice broke in, "there is nothing to be gained by shouting like that."

Mr. Bodoni tore his gaze away from the glittering eyes, and saw for the first time that there was another passenger within. It was a man with a bruised face and rumpled hair, wearing a very old-fashioned suit that was torn in several places and mottled with large wet stains.

The woman turned and jabbed at him with her umbrella, like a lion-tamer forcing an unruly beast back into its corner. "You, sir," she shouted, "are a scoundrel! I believe the most appropriate place for *you* is a police station. I intend to see you taken to one at the earliest opportunity." She turned to Mr. Bodoni again. "Don't stand there like an imbecile, my man! I have vitally important duties to discharge and I wish to return to them at once! Do you understand the mechanism of this conveyance?"

"Hah?"

"Look here, my good fellow," the man said from the corner of the elevator. He had been staring at the washing machines against the wall. "Just tell us where we are, will you?"

"Yeah," Mr. Bodoni said. "Here."

"No, no, what I mean is, where is this building—?"

"I wish to return!" the woman shouted at Mr. Bodoni. "Do what is necessary this instant, or I shall seek out your employer and have your wages stopped for a month!"

"Madame," the man snapped, "you are sorely trying my patience. Something serious is happening here, and I am trying to find out what, but you keep inter—"

"*Patience*, you scum!" she roared. "If I could stand, I'd show you patience!" She turned and slashed at him with her umbrella. The steel tip grazed his vest. A button fell to the floor and rolled over to Mr. Bodoni's feet. She turned back to skewer him with her glare. "I—wish—to—go—back," she said, enunciating each word like the crack of a whip. "I am waiting."

The message penetrated at last. Mr. Bodoni jerked his thumb toward the ceiling. "You wanna go back, hah?

Back up there?"

She closed her eyes and inclined her head slightly. "*So* intelligent of him!" she murmured. "*Such* a firm grasp of what is required! *If* you will be so kind as to set me in motion."

Mr. Bodoni saw that for some reason she was waiting for him to press the button. He sidled toward the elevator, keeping his gaze fixed on her umbrella. Her mouth tightened, and she drew in the skirt of her robe as he approached. He dared not ask her which floor she wanted. He reached inside and pressed the first button his fingers found.

It was the emergency button. They all gave a start as the warning bell on top of the elevator burst into a deafening clangor. "Stop that noise!" the woman shouted, pounding Mr. Bodoni's paunch with her umbrella. He pressed three other buttons simultaneously and staggered back. The bell stopped. Its echoes could be heard bouncing about and dying away in the shaft.

"Look here!" the man said, appealing to Mr. Bodoni with a wild eye. "What do you know about this?"

"Not dangerous," Mr. Bodoni croaked.

The door trundled shut.

Mr. Bodoni sagged against the wall. Beads of sweat were trickling down his cheeks and neck. "Crazy!" he muttered. "Boy oh boy—crazy! Whew! Must be the heat." He found that his legs were shaking. He collapsed into his camp chair, took a deep swig of beer, and fanned himself with the sports section of his paper. Who? Who? Who . . . ? They weren't tenants, he knew that. He hoped they weren't *going* to be tenants. Boy oh boy, with a crazy lady like that in the building he'd have to get a job somewhere else . . . Maybe they just wandered in from the street, crazy from the temperature. He hoped 'they would wander out again. He listened. All was quiet. Boy oh boy . . . He finished his beer in two more gulps, leaned over to retrieve the scattered comics—and froze.

Bang bang bang bang!

The elevator was coming down again. The shaft resounded like a huge drum to the blows of her umbrella.

Mr. Bodoni's spirit failed. "Nah!" he bleated. His camp chair clattered over backward as he scrambled to his feet. He fled toward the stairs on the opposite side of the basement, shedding pages of newspaper as he went. Behind him the elevator door opened. Her shriek stabbed through his ears: *"Imbecile! Return me at once!"* He soared up the steps like a kangaroo.

He was standing out on the front sidewalk, panting and mopping his face, when a hand fell on his shoulder.

"Nah!" he cried, leaping halfway across Ward Street in one bound.

"Hey, Bodoni, whatsa matter with you? It's me!"

He turned, and saw that it was an old acquaintance, a man who lived on the sixth floor.

"Listen, the elevator's stuck down in the basement. I keep punching the button but nothing happens. It won't come up."

"Leave alone!" Mr. Bodoni cried. "Crazy lady in there!"

"What?"

Mr. Bodoni told him what had happened, and invited him to come see for himself. They crept silently a little way down the basement stairs, and peered across the room. The elevator stood open-doored, with only one occupant now. She sat on the floor with folded arms, an implacable presence, radiating fury in almost visible waves.

The two men sneaked back up the stairs.

"Oh boy oh boy!" Mr. Bodoni moaned. "What to do?"

"We better call the cops, Bodoni. She oughta be in a psychiatric ward."

It took three policemen to get her away. After the din was over, Mr. Bodoni discovered that the elevator had made its final trip.

❧ ❧ ❧ ❧ ❧ ❧

"Crazy!" he said to me now. "Everyting all at once! Motor shot! Circuits burnt out! Cable busted! Boy oh boy—zap!" He took a deep breath and grinned. "I'm gonna play bocce ball inna park. See ya!"

My mental turmoil of the last two days and nights was nothing compared to now. Because while Mr. Bodoni had been talking, a feeling that I can only call recognition had flashed over me. That "crazy lady," with her stout figure and glittering eyes and pince-nez glasses and umbrella, sounded so much like—like—! Why not? It wasn't impossible! And there was a man with her, too . . . Now who on earth—?

Oh lord, *what had happened in 1881?*

There was no relief in the park, no relief. I trudged back to the apartment building and hauled myself up five weary flights of stairs and mixed myself a cold drink. Susan's diary was on my bookshelves where I had put it day before yesterday. I looked at its spine and shook my head, almost wishing that the whole baffling business had never begun. There was something sticking up out of the top, like a marker. I couldn't remember having put any such thing in the diary. I pulled the book out to check. Yes. Something bulky between the front cover and first page . . . Brown paper . . .

Funny! I stared at it and turned it over in my hands for a long time before the meaning of it began to sink in. It was a large folded envelope of time-darkened brittle paper. The words on it were still perfectly clear: SUSAN SHAW—MR. SHAW—DON'T COME DOWN and on the other side of the fold UNTIL YOU READ WHAT'S INSIDE! Inside, darkened to a burnt orange-brown, was a fragile folded sheet of newspaper . . .

The back of my neck began to prickle. Now I really know how Susan and Victoria and Robert had felt when, after finding the treasure, they discovered that the front page of their newspaper had changed. My word! It's one thing to mention "time paradox" glibly, as I had to Charles, and another thing altogether to *experience* it. I shivered. Here was the paradox in my hands, beyond explanation, beyond argument. The envelope had been in the diary for many decades. There was a straight-edged stain on the first page and the inside of the cover to prove it. But there had been no stain and no envelope in the diary day before yesterday, because I had not yet sent the envelope up the elevator to change the past . . .

Wait a minute—!

Mightn't that mean that the diary—that the diary also—that in the diary—?

My legs were doing funny things. I had to sit down. My mouth was dry and my hands shook as I turned the pages to the place where—

Yes! There were now pages and pages of fast loopy scrawl after the word "despair"!

⨾{ 13. MRS. WALKER WEEPS }⨿

It's happened! It's happened! We called up
the elevator to leave and there was a sign on
the back wall. At first we thought it was
one of Mr. Bodoni's, but when my eyes got
used to the light I saw it had our names on
it! It said to read it before we came down,
and because I tried to, it happened at
last . . .

"Think an eagle will be enough?" Mr. Shaw said. "We
never did find out what they charge, did we?"

"No," Susan murmured.

"Let's see . . . We've been here two days, more or
less—oh, nuts! I don't know why I'm making a fuss
about it. Let's just leave all we've got." The coins clinked
as he laid them out on the little table by his bed.

He tiptoed over to the window and looked out. All the
lights in the Walkers' house—all that were visible from
here—had been extinguished for nearly an hour. That
should be sufficient time for them to be settled into sleep
over there. The Hollisters, who had retired about an hour
ago, were well settled themselves; a throbbing chorus of
snorts and snores from the back of the house attested
to that.

"All right, chick," he said. "Time to go. Got everything?"

She picked up her diary and the farewell letter to
Victoria and Robert, and nodded miserably. He blew out
the candle, and when their eyes had become adjusted to
the dark they crept down the stairs.

The stars seemed even more brilliant than night before last; the sky was luminous with them. 'I'll never see stars like this again,' she thought. They blurred. She stumbled along beside her father, blind with tears.

"Front door? Back door?" he murmured.

Her only wish now was to get the pain over with as quickly as possible. "Front," she choked.

Mr. Shaw stopped when they reached the porch steps. "Shoes!" he whispered, pantomiming the removal of his boots; he wasn't going to take any chances in the house. They sat down on the bottom step and took off their shoes—his genuine American articles, and the button-ups she had borrowed from Victoria. 'I'll leave them behind,' she thought. 'Nothing I can do about the dress, though.' Not so long ago she had day-dreamed about going to town with Victoria and buying a whole wardrobe . . . The memory wrenched her heart.

They crept up to the front door in their stocking feet. Mr. Shaw opened it with extreme caution. Silence closed around them inside, broken only by their own breathing and the muffled ticking of the grandfather clock. They felt their way step by step among the dim shapes of parlor furniture. Here was the curtained doorway through which Maggie had made her appearance this morning. "Time—time—time" the clock dirged as they passed by.

"All right, Susie," Mr. Shaw whispered, "call it up."

She put her farewell letter on the table, propping it against the stuffed owl's glass bell, and placed Victoria's shoes side by side underneath. The lump in her throat felt as large as a fist. She turned quickly to the wainscotting of the outer wall, and pressed her thumb against the warm wooden surface. She could feel the vibration of the faraway mechanism lurching into life.

Her shoulders began to shake. Mr. Shaw murmured and put his arm around her. They waited. Behind the paneling sounded a hum, an approaching muffled groan . . . The wainscotting split, and rumbled apart. They flinched under the glare of the electric light.

There was a new sign attached to the rear wall of the elevator, but their eyes were so dazzled that they couldn't make out the words. Another one of Mr. Bodoni's notices, no doubt, about "smokking" in the elevator or dropping "liter" on its floor . . .

They got in.

Her aching eyes were beginning to accomodate to the light. SUSAN SHAW, she read on the new sign. Her mind was so numb with grief that she did not recognize these words for an instant. MR. SHAW . . .

"*Daddy!*" she whispered.

He already had his finger on the third-floor button. He had not looked twice at the sign.

"*No!*" she whisper-shouted, seizing his hand and pulling it away from the bank of buttons.

"What are you doing?" he muttered.

"Look, look, look!" She pulled him around by the arm so that he was forced to see the sign again.

SUSAN SHAW—MR. SHAW—DON'T COME DOWN UNTIL YOU READ WHAT'S INSIDE!

They stared, too astonished to move.

"What's that all about?" Mr. Shaw murmured after a moment. "Inside what?"

"I don't know," she whispered.

"Do you think one of the Walker kids—?"

"No. The elevator wouldn't come up for them. It must be—" The idea was incredible, but she could think of no alternative. "It must be from the twentieth century!" And as she said it, the answer came to her.

Robert and Victoria had been successful after all.

She stepped forward and tore the sign from the wall. It was not a sign, but a manila envelope. Inside . . . She tried to force her finger under the glued-down flap.

The elevator door sighed, and began to trundle shut.

With a squeak of fright she hurled herself at the door, caught it just in time, and forced it back. It began to bunt against her hand with convulsive little leaps.

"Get out, get out!" she whispered to her father. "We have to read this."

"Why can't we read it going down?" he said.

"*No*. It says don't go down until *after* we read it!"

"But—"

"Oh!" she cried—tried to cry; her voice was too choked with urgency to sound very loud. She let the bucking door go, flung herself on him, and yanked him out into the hallway with a strength she had never suspected in herself. The wainscotting closed up again, the elevator groaned away down the shaft, and they were left clinging together and panting in the dark.

"Susan," he said in a low dangerous voice, "I am at the end of my patience with you. I have had all the frustrations I am able to cope with. Call that elevator back."

"Daddy, I will, but I have to read this first!"

"Just how the *devil* do you propose to read anything in this dark?"

"I—" she began, casting desperately about, "I— Candles!" She started to back down the hallway. "There're candles on the mantelpiece in the parlor."

"Susan, you—"

"Daddy, just a minute, *please!*"

She turned and hurried as quickly as the dark permitted back to the parlor. Ooop! She found herself bending double over a hassock or something that had caught her on the shins; fortunately it was well padded. She looked about. Her eyes were adjusting to the darkness again. A shape loomed nearby. She touched smooth wood and plush—it was the sofa. And there, dimly gleaming a few yards away, was the white marble of the fireplace.

Somewhere at the other end of the house a door opened.

She whirled around toward the doorway and went rigid. Voices murmured and a light flickered on the other side, in the hallway where her father— He was going to be caught flat-footed!

Unless it was Victoria and Robert, in which case—

It was not Victoria and Robert. The voices were different. Two voices—one weeping, one murmuring . . .

They were almost in the parlor. Candlelight wavered through the portieres, shadows swayed on the parlor rug. Susan broke out of her paralysis. For some reason her father hadn't been seen. She mustn't be seen either. She scurried behind an armchair and crouched. But the urge to look could not be resisted, and she straightened up again until her eyes were just above the back of the chair.

Through the doorway came Mrs. Walker in a white peignoir, stumbling, weeping. "I can't bear it," she sobbed. "Oh, I can't bear any more!" Her loosened waist-length hair tumbled about her face, half hiding it. In candlelight it no longer looked chestnut, but dark, nearly black. The effect was both ravishingly beautiful and heart-breaking. Susan groaned to herself, and gripped the back of the sofa.

Maggie trotted along next to Mrs. Walker, supporting her with one arm. She held the candlestick in her free hand. "Ah, sure, sure now," she murmured. "It'll be all right, Mum. Sure, now." They slowly passed through the parlor into the front hall, and paused, out of Susan's sight now, at the foot of the staircase.

"Isabelle!" said Cousin Jane's voice from upstairs.

The candlelight flickered violently. Mrs. Walker murmured a wordless reply.

"We have much to accomplish tomorrow, Isabelle," Cousin Jane's voice crackled. "I suggest that you come up to bed immediately and obtain a full night's sleep. Wandering about at this late hour is not conducive to good health, and sets a bad example. Is Maggie with you?"

"Yes . . ."

"Have you locked up the house for the night, Maggie?"

The candlelight flickered again. "Sure, Mum, and

wasn't I jist on the edge of doin' it when ye asked me."

"In other words, you have *not* done it. Lock up at once, and then get to bed! I hope I shall not have to tell you twice tomorrow night. Come up, Isabelle."

"Lock up, is it?" Maggie muttered. The bolt on the front door banged into place. "There, ye black-hearted she-divel! As for the rest of it, ye may do it yerself. I draw me wages for housekeepin', not guardin' a jail."

"Good night, Isabelle!" Cousin Jane said. It was not a wish, but a command. Doors closed. Maggie, still muttering in a fierce undertone, trudged upstairs. The candlelight faded, and all downstairs was dark again.

Susan stood up and groped her way back to the hall. "Daddy?" she whispered.

The curtains by the window stirred. "Here!" he whispered.

"They didn't see you?"

"No, I zipped behind here and they went right by. I saw *her*, though. Good night!"

Something about him felt different. A kind of electric tenseness radiated from him; but it wasn't the anger and frustration of their recent quarrel over the elevator. Not now . . .

"Crying!" he muttered to himself. "Good lord! She was crying . . ."

She didn't know what to say. They stood there for several minutes. He seemed to be holding his breath, or caught up in a trance.

At last he breathed out with a sharp sound, almost a snort. He whispered, "All right, chick, let's go."

She became aware that she was still holding the manila envelope. "Daddy," she whispered, "we haven't read the message yet."

"Never mind that! Later!"

"But—"

He seized her arm with such a grip that she almost yelped with pain, and began propelling her toward the place where the elevator door was.

And past it.

And through the parlor.

And out the front door, whose bolt and knob yielded as silently and easily to him as if magic had been in his touch; and across the porch; and down the front walk.

"Daddy," she whispered, scarcely able to get the words out, "are we staying?"

"Absolutely!"

Then, in the middle of Ward Lane, he stopped again, and let go of her arm, and fell into that trance-like state.

"By *George!*" he burst out after a moment. "I never even looked at her before! Never even saw her! I mean, all the time she was right in front of my eyes, and I never—Oh, good lord!"

Susan was in something of a trance herself. The smell of the night air, the brilliance of the stars, were too sweet to bear. Something inside her went *pop*, a warm bubbly explosion. Hello, stars! They blurred again—but this time through tears of happiness.

"Oh, Daddy . . . !" she choked.

"What?" he said, starting out of his reverie. "What's that? Oh, yes! Well, come on."

Again he seized her arm in that powerful grip. She let out a squeak. He paid no heed, but swept her back to the Hollisters' so rapidly that she had to half-run to stay on her feet. The symphony of snores changed its pace for a measure or two, as they crept up the stairs, and then continued *a tempo*.

She put her diary and the envelope down, and felt around the bureau top until she found a match, and lit the candle. Mr. Shaw stood in the soft yellow light looking down with a puzzled expression at his boots—which were dangling by their laces from his left hand. She noticed now that she was in stocking-feet, too; her shoes—Victoria's—were still under the little table in the hallway of the Walkers' house . . . Not that it mattered. Not that anything mattered now!

"I never felt a thing!" she laughed. "We've been walking on air!"

"Ah," he said profoundly. He sat down on the edge of his bed, and was lost to the world again.

Susan tore open the manila envelope, and pulled out a folded piece of newspaper. Houses for sale. Houses for rent . . . She turned the paper over and saw a crayoned circle. *REWARD for info. leading to contact with Jane Hildegarde Clamp* . . . Question mark in crayon. Familiar name . . . Oh, she couldn't concentrate! A fit of giggles took possession of her. She kept looking at her father, who sat there muttering "By George!" to himself, with a dazed look on his face.

Suddenly he stood up, strode over to her, and kissed her on the forehead.

"Susie," he said, "thank you. Thank you very, very much. It all makes sense now. I mean, the whole thing. You knew it all along, didn't you? It's just that I couldn't see it until . . . But I mean it makes *sense* now. What I mean is—do you know what I mean?"

"Yes," she said, laughing up into his lunatic face. "I know what you mean."

⊰⊱ 14. MR. SWINGLE STATES HIS BUSINESS ⊱⊰

> *. . . tried to figure out what that notice in the newspaper meant. Was the name just a coincidence? While we were talking about it somebody came to call on us. He was a man with a beard, named Arbuthnot Swingle. The moment I saw him I knew he looked familiar . . .*

Mr. Shaw's behavior at breakfast was so remarkable that even Mrs. Hollister forgot her shyness long enough to look at him directly, instead of out of the corner of her eye. At one moment he would be gay and laughing, delighted with everything. Abruptly he would plunge into a fit of abstraction; his eyes would glaze over, and with a look almost of gloom he would poke at his eggs and bacon. Just as abruptly, his eyes would crinkle into a smile again, and with a great laugh he would attack his breakfast like a man recently rescued from starvation.

Susan giggled, and choked over her toast, and stuffed herself, and giggled again. She was acting as loony as Daddy! Mrs. Hollister's lips tightened as she pushed the coffee pot toward them. She looked as though she suspected them of having taken a pre-breakfast nip of spirits! Susan doubled over with uncontrollable giggling.

After breakfast they went upstairs. Mr. Shaw paused at the door of his room, and collapsed against the jamb.

"Susie," he groaned, "how can I ask her to marry me? I haven't got a thing to offer!"

"You have too! You're handsome and kind and—"

"And I'm flat broke, or right on the edge of it. Look!"

They went into his room, and he pointed at the handful of coins on the night table. "There's our fortune—and we probably owe most of it to the Hollisters. We have what's left, plus the clothes we stand in."

"Plus our intelligence," she added. "We're both awfully smart, Daddy. And our knowledge! We know lots that people these days don't."

"Mmm . . . But that may not be the advantage you think it is. What I know best, for instance, is how to keep track of corporate finances. But I do it with machines that probably haven't been invented yet."

"Maybe you could invent them!"

"Oh, chick!" he laughed. "I'm not the Connecticut Yankee . . ." He sat in a wobbly rocking chair and put his chin in his hand. "The point is, I'm going to have to earn a living, but I don't know how to make my way around in this century. It's like being in a foreign country. I know I'm capable of learning my way around eventually, but it takes time; and while I'm doing it—" he pointed again at the money on the table "—that's what we have to live on . . . Sure wish I knew what happened to that treasure!"

"So do I," she sighed. "There's something funny about that. *I* don't think it was a tramp with a dog, or boys looking for nests."

"Well, whatever it was . . ." He lifted his hands and let them drop. "If I knew anybody here, I could borrow some money to tide us over. But I don't. And good night!" he cried, "all this is based on the supposition that Isabelle is willing to accept me in the first place. How are we even going to *see* her again, with that Clamp monster standing in the way?"

"Don't worry, Daddy. Bobbie and Vicky got around her yesterday, and so can we. Oh! Clamp! I almost forgot!" She ran into her room and brought back the piece of newspaper. "Here—Bobbie and Vicky asked the witch for help, and we got this in the elevator."

"What? What witch?"

She explained.

He began to laugh and shake his head. "You kids are—amazing! The way you accept . . . !"

"It's just a matter of getting used to it, Daddy. Here, read this. It's weird. I can't figure it out."

"Hmm," he said, after looking at the circled item for a while. "Is Cousin Jane's middle name Hildegarde?"

"I don't know."

"Who the devil would be looking for *her*, anyway? I should think almost anybody in the world would be happy *not* to know where she is."

"But look, Daddy—what's so weird about it is that it's a twentieth-century paper. I think."

"What! Mm—no date; top's been torn off. You're right, though, it does look like a—yes, see, it says 'blood plasma' here. That's twentieth century, all right. The name must be a coincidence, then—they can't be talking about *our* Clamp. Worse luck!"

"Why worse luck?"

"Because think how convenient it would be if she *were* in the twentieth—"

There was a timid knock.

Mrs. Hollister stood squirming in the hall when Susan opened the door. "Gentleman to see you," she murmured at the ceiling.

"Me?"

"Well, no, both of you. He says it's kind of important, could you spare the time right now?" And Mrs. Hollister, looking hard at her own feet, handed Susan a card.

She studied it in bewilderment. Slowly untangling

119

each Gothic letter from the thicket of ornament in which it lay concealed, she deciphered the name: Arbuthnot Swingle.

With a shrug she gave the card to her father.

"Who's this?" he asked Mrs. Hollister.

"I don't know, sir," she mumbled at the door lintel. "Gentleman with a beard . . ."

It was Mr. Shaw's turn to shrug. "Beard . . . ? Oh, well, all right, send him up."

Mrs. Hollister departed, and the Shaws frowned at each other.

There was a firm, quiet knock, and the caller stood in the doorway. He had an untidy, bushy black beard, and his suit was rumpled as though it had been slept in. By way of contrast, his hair was impeccably combed with oil or pomade, and glistened like the feathers of a blackbird. He was holding a derby in his white hands.

"I hope that my visit is not inopportune," he said. Susan started at the sound of that low, smooth voice. There was something familiar about it . . .

"No, no," Mr. Shaw said. "Come in, Mr., uh, Swingle. Have a seat."

Mr. Swingle laid his derby on the floor with care, then sat down, crossed his legs, and looked at Susan—and smiled. It was a curious smile, combining admiration with an undertone of irony. Susan squirmed a little, but could not stop staring at this unsettling stranger.

"Your daughter, sir?" Mr. Swingle enquired, turning to Mr. Shaw.

"That's right—my daughter Susan. My name is Shaw."

"Ah, yes, I was informed of that fact by your excellent landlady. Well, Mr. Shaw, I congratulate you: your daughter, sir, is an artist of the first rank. You yourself have a professional ability that is practically unbeatable. Practically—but not quite . . . Will you join me in a cigar, sir?"

"No, thanks, I don't—"

"I hope it will not incommode you if I indulge in one myself?"

"No, go ahead. I don't catch your meaning, Mr. Swingle. Will you explain?"

But Mr. Swingle, having lit his cigar, turned again toward Susan with that admiring and ironic smile. And as she noticed the way he held his cigar, lightly, fastidiously, between his fingertips, her eyes began to widen and her mouth dropped open.

"Ah, ah, ah!" he said, holding up his other hand and forestalling her gasp. "Such sharp eyes! Such lightning recognition! You are quite correct, my dear—we have met before."

And with an even wider smile than ever, he tore off his beard.

"Mr. Sweeney!" she moaned.

"Exactly! Or should I say, more or less? We know how convenient it is to have numerous names, don't we? Algernon Sweeney will do—or Arbuthnot Swingle, or even Abernathy Swinnerton, if you prefer." Wrinkling his nose, he dropped the beard beside his hat. "Pah! What a tiresome apparatus! However, I did not wish to be recognized by the Walkers or by our good landlady. But I was sure that *your* keen eyes would not be deceived for long, my dear!"

"Will you kindly tell us what all this is about, Mr. Swingle—Sweeney—whatever?" Mr. Shaw said.

"With pleasure, sir. Your plan to exclude me from the kill was audacious and beautifully executed. It almost succeeded, but not quite. So I am here to congratulate you on a good try, and to inform you that it has failed. I am also here to demand my share of the spoils yet to come."

"Kill?" Mr. Shaw said. "Spoils? I don't—"

"Oh, come, come, my dear Shaw! I see that your acting abilities are almost equal to the young lady's. That air of innocent bafflement is marvelously well done! But why waste it on me? I believe we understand each other."

"The understanding seems to be more on your side than mine," Mr. Shaw said.

Mr. Sweeney blew a cloud of smoke toward the ceiling. "You need some time to think, don't you? Well, think away!—I'll give you all the time you need. Meanwhile, I will be as plain as I can. Through some coincidence we have settled upon the same mark, you and I. I do not intend to retire from the field. You do not intend to retire from the field. Therefore, we must share the mark between us."

"Mark?"

"Please don't be tiresome, Shaw! I refer, or course, to our mutual victim, Isabelle Walker."

"Ah-h-h!" Mr. Shaw said. His eyes narrowed. "Victim? Good lord, man, you don't think that I—"

"No, I don't think," Mr. Sweeney said, waving his hand. "I know. And now that I know, I am not going to be put off the way I was last time. I confess that I was absolutely taken in by that little masquerade you arranged for me. It must have given you a good deal of amusement to see me fleeing from here under the conviction that Isabelle had already been picked clean and that I was in mortal danger of smallpox. Well, I don't begrudge you your little laugh. We know how to be philosophical in this game, don't we? And anyway, I had another little operation in town to fall back on."

"What do you mean by that?" Mr. Shaw asked.

"Another widow," Mr. Sweeney sighed. "Elderly, plain, grateful for a little attention—you know the sort of thing. Such a routine job that I could scarcely suppress my yawns as I relieved her of everything. A paltry fifteen hundred. *So* tedious . . . But, one must live, mustn't one?"

"You took—*every*thing?"

"My dear Shaw, what a curious question! Of course I did. After all, she has her house, and a large supply of leisure. She can take in boarders, or do laundry, or something."

"Oh. Yes, I see . . . ." Mr. Shaw clasped his hands together until the knuckles turned white. "Well, ah, what brought you back here?"

"Why, I saw the two of you at the railroad station, just after the conclusion of my business with the widow. It seemed strange that the 'servant girl,' whom I had last seen in tears"—Mr. Sweeney smiled at Susan—"should now be so happily hobnobbing with a gentleman. I thought it warranted further investigation. So I boarded the train, walked rapidly through the cars to the last one, disembarked, and took shelter behind a convenient coal bin. From there I watched the servant girl and gentleman being conveyed out of town by a citizen with a surrey. When the citizen returned, I treated him to some beer—a great deal of beer—and learned some interesting facts: that the servant girl and gentleman were father and daughter, or at any rate passed themselves off as such; that they were boarding at Hollisters', right next door to the Walkers; and that the Walkers, far from having succumbed to smallpox, were in excellent health!

"Well, all this seemed to be worth looking into! I took a little stroll into the country, and sat down in the shade to observe the passing scene. And what an interesting scene it was! Here is the former servant girl, now a young lady, mixing on the closest terms with the Walker children. And, a little later, here she comes with her father, walking out to take the air and to commune with Nature. How absorbing Nature is to them! They listen to the songs of birds; they observe the flight of butterflies; they study the—oh, let us say 'minerals', under a certain blackberry bush—"

"Oh!" Susan gasped.

"Oh!" Mr. Sweeney echoed with a brilliant smile. "The study of Nature is so *rewarding,* isn't it?"

"Oh!" Susan ground out through clenched teeth. "You—!"

"Susan!" Mr. Shaw said, quietly but with such intensity that she turned toward him at once. He was trying to tell her something with his eyes. "Susan, my dear, Mr. Sweeney is right—we must know how to be philosophical in this game. Sit down, please, and be philosophical."

She subsided, wondering what he was up to.

"Well, Sweeney," Mr. Shaw continued. "We've had our little laugh, and now you're having yours. You are a dangerous man, I see."

"Permit me to return the compliment, sir. As soon as you had left, and I had discovered the gold, I did nothing but sing your praises for five minutes. '*What* a smooth operation!' I said. '*What* a pair of artists!' But a question began to nag me as I observed you further. A professional usually departs quickly after making such a kill— but here you were, showing every intention of remaining in the vicinity! What could be the reason for that? The answer staggered me, sir, and my admiration for your audacity soared beyond bounds. You could only be lingering here because there was even *more* to be gotten out of Isabelle Walker."

"Mmm," Mr. Shaw said. "You know, it's fascinating to watch your powerful line of reasoning unfold."

"You flatter me, sir. Well, enough of compliments. Shall we get down to business? I have a proposition to make."

Mr. Shaw raised his eyebrows.

"I propose to help you, if you wish, in finishing off Isabelle. Or, if you prefer, I will stand aside while you do it yourself."

"Very generous of you, Sweeney. You, ah, have a price, of course?"

"Of course. I expect half of what is to come."

"Oh, you do. And what about my gold?"

Mr. Sweeney smiled and shook his head. "I keep that, of course. If money is to be carelessly strewn about the countryside, then it must belong to him who finds it."

"I see. Now, let me get this straight—I'm having some trouble swallowing this. You propose to steal, and keep, all the money we have gotten so far; and you also propose to rob us of half of whatever *else* we can get. Is that it?"

"Your terms are crude, but their sense is correct."

Mr. Shaw's smile was incredulous. "Talk—about—audacity!" he said. "Sweeney, you flaming idiot, what on earth makes you think I'd ever consider a fool proposition like that?"

"My dear Shaw, let's not be obtuse, shall we? You don't have any choice. I've caught you red-handed, as they say in those lurid boys' novels. Isabelle may not know yet that her money has disappeared, or she may

125

believe that you are 'investing' it for her; but in either case I can cause her to begin asking tiresome questions. It would be amusing to denounce you to the police, also. And while you are trying to calm their suspicions on one hand, and Isabelle's on the other, and failing, and finding yourself under arraignment on a very serious charge —*I* will be quietly traveling to distant parts with well-lined pockets . . . Now, surely, forgetting what you have lost, and sharing a mere half of what is to come, must be more attractive to you than *that*."

Oh, the absurd, dreadful scoundrel, with his total misunderstanding of the situation and his silly, empty threats! Susan could no longer contain herself. She broke out in angry, disbelieving laughter.

"Susan!" Mr. Shaw snapped; and then, sending her that cryptic message with his eyes again, "Philosophy, my dear. Philosophy!" His shoulders slumped. He raised his hand to his mouth. "Well, Sweeney," he mumbled. "I—ah . . . I guess I—I need some time to think."

"Of course," Mr. Sweeney said smoothly. "I understand. Think as much as you need to."

There was a long silence. Susan wondered what her father was up to. He looked so beaten, sitting there with a glazed look in his eyes and his chin in his hands; as if all of Mr. Sweeney's assumptions were true! And yet Mr. Sweeney was wrong about *everything*, and in such an awful, hateful way. Oh, how she detested him! Look at him sitting there, so calm and easy, blowing his smoke at the ceiling with a little smile! She clenched her fists and bit the inside of her lip.

At last Mr. Shaw sighed and said, "Well, Sweeney, you seem to be holding a loaded pistol at my head . . . I guess I have to say yes to your proposal."

"I thought you would take a rational view," Mr.

Sweeney purred. "Now, do you need my assistance or not? Where does your operation stand at present?"

Mr. Shaw leaned back in his chair and studied the cracks in the ceiling plaster. "Wel-l-l," he said at last, pursing his lips, "I think we'd better go ahead by ourselves, if you don't mind. Less complicated that way. You see, the fact is that we're on the verge of success. Your reasoning was correct, Sweeney. There *is* more where that gold came from—much more. And our hands are almost on it."

"Ah!" Mr. Sweeney breathed. "Cash? Investments? Property?"

"Uh, jewelry," Mr. Shaw said. He spoke slowly and carefully. "Mrs. Walker's late husband was extravagant, and used to—to shower her with jewelry on every occasion. Which, as you know, she never wears. She puts on a very, ah, modest appearance."

"Yes, she does, doesn't she?" Mr. Sweeney said, nodding. "I must say it made it difficult for me to assess how much she was good for. I never suspected jewelry."

"I wouldn't have, either, if it hadn't been for Susan. You see, we, ah, specialize in widows with children. You can get a lot of valuable information from children—if you're a child yourself. That's where Susan comes in. As you know, she's gained the complete confidence of Robert and Victoria. They put on little plays for their own amusement. They dress up in Mama's and Papa's old clothes, you know, and Susie suggests putting on jewels to make it more realistic. They can't resist that. It's so naughty—they have to, ah, borrow the key to Mama's jewel case without her knowing about it. But safe, too, because nothing gets lost and it's all put away when the theatricals are over. And meanwhile, during the course of the play, Susan appraises the stuff—she's been to school for that—and when she gets the opportunity she makes a wax impression of the key."

"Ah!" Mr. Sweeney said. "*What* an artist! How much will it come to?"

Mr. Shaw assumed a reluctant expression.

"Oh, come, Shaw, don't drag your feet with me. I'm going to find out sooner or later, you know."

"Well, ah, we're pretty confident that it will be between, oh, forty and fifty thousand."

"Ah!" Mr. Sweeney breathed. His eyes were glittering. "I'll want to appraise them myself, of course, when we—" and he made a clutching gesture. "How soon do you think—?"

"Well . . . the situation over there is delicate. Mrs. Walker's cousin is visiting, and I'm sorry to say that she regards me with suspicion. I'm sure I don't know why!" Mr. Sweeney smiled his appreciation of this joke. "So we have to work a little faster than is usually convenient. Susan rejoins her friends this morning, and she'll see to it that there are more amateur theatricals. If she can, she will make an impression of the key. We have a tentative plan to go on from there, but it will depend on what happens this morning, of course. Tell you what. Where are you staying? I could come and give you a progress report, say about twelve-thirty."

"Now, Shaw, you know I have no intention of divulging the whereabouts of my present lodgings. Let's meet in the Hollisters' stable. Twelve-thirty will be suitable. Have you anything else to say to me?"

Mr. Shaw shook his head.

"Very well." Mr. Sweeney picked up his beard, looked at it with an expression of distaste, and re-attached it to his chin. "This is the last time I intend to burden my face with this—excrescence. Hollisters' stable at twelve-thirty, then. No, no, do not see me down the stairs. I prefer you to remain here. If you have any idea of following me, dismiss it; the minute I suspect myself of being spied upon, I will denounce you to the police. Good morning, sir; good morning, Miss Shaw. Remember!"

He paused in the doorway, pointed his fingertip at the side of his head, pistol-fashion, gave them a dazzling smile, and was gone.

⊰⊱ 15. IN THE DRAGON'S LAIR ⊰⊱

> *. . . so furious he scared me. After he got it out of his system he told me why he had put on that act with Mr. Sweeney and what he had in mind. The first thing was to get hold of Bobbie. We couldn't waste any time, so I had to sneak into the Walkers' house . . .*

When they heard his footsteps on the veranda, Mr. Shaw jumped up and strode to the front window. His face was white, and as he watched Mr. Sweeney's retreating figure his jaw muscles twitched. He watched in silence for a moment, then turned, and with a roar fell on his bed and pounded it with his fists until the springs jangled and clouds of dust eddied throughout the room.

"Oh, the weasel!" he shouted. "The dirty cur! The slimy low-down cockroach!"

Gradually he subsided, and sat panting on the floor.

"Oh, good night!" he groaned. "I think I could tear that skunk to little pieces and stamp on them! Calling her Isabelle! *Isabelle!* I don't know how I kept from grabbing his throat each time he said that. Oh, the rat!"

"That was an incredible act you put on with him, Daddy."

"Hunh! I could hardly believe I was doing it myself. Maybe some of your talent is rubbing off on me!"

"But what was it for?"

"To gain time. Say, we shouldn't be here. He's probably going to be spying on us again soon. I guess he hides in the trees across the road, but I don't know. Come on!"

He seized her arm and hurried her downstairs, through the kitchen and back shed, and out to the stable. Chickens fled before them, clucking. They sat down on a sack of oats.

"We have to get hold of Bobbie," Mr. Shaw muttered, biting his lip.

"Daddy, what are you up to with that fantastic story about putting on plays with Mrs. Walker's jewels?"

"I told you, I need time to think. That dirty swine has our fortune. If I didn't play along with him he'd vanish with it. It's just lucky for us that he has this greasy little fantasy about what we're up to. It means that as long as I tell him what he wants to hear, he'll keep coming back. Listen, we need Bobbie. Do you think you can penetrate the dragon's lair and get hold of him and bring him here?"

"I can try. Why do we—?"

"Oh, I'll explain later. It's just an idea I'm beginning to have . . . Now don't let yourself be seen from the road, chick, and tell Bobbie the same. The less Sweeney knows about our movements, the better. Got it?"

"Yes."

"Good luck, then. And listen—there's *got* to be a way out of this. I'm going to be thinking hard about it while you're gone. Bring 'im back alive!"

He hugged and kissed her, and she slipped out of the stable.

The thing to do, since she must not be seen from the road, was to approach the Walkers' house from the rear. Robert and Victoria had done it yesterday by following the hedge back. She walked behind the stable, wincing with each step. She was still in stocking feet.

Behind the stable was a weedy pasture. A huge grey-and-white barred hen looked at her with a malevolent eye, and sidled off, clucking. There—the hedge rounded away toward the Walkers' side. She followed it, sucking air in through her teeth each time she stepped on a stick or stone. And here, finally, was a gate in the hedge, and on the other side was the back of the Walkers' stable.

She peered around the corner of the stable, and saw that a sun parlor window was open—probably the one Robert had used yesterday. There was no consistent cover between here and there. The only thing to do was make a dash for the hydrangeas under the window.

She dashed.

No one had seen her. She threw herself under the shrubbery, and crouched, panting. The soles of her feet throbbed.

A heavy greenhouse smell drifted out of the window. By standing on her toes she could just look over the sill into a bright room full of wicker furniture and potted plants. She listened. Somewhere in the house she could hear a clinking of plates and an occasional murmur of voices. They must be at breakfast, then; but where, she couldn't tell. Far enough from the sun parlor, anyway, to judge by the sounds.

She heaved herself up and slithered in, banging her knees as she passed over the sill, and landing on a basket-work chaise longue that creaked loudly under her weight.

The breakfast sounds continued without pause.

Peeking around the door frame, she discovered that she was looking into a hallway—not the one that contained the elevator, but the wider one on the other side of the house. A quick dash would take her to the stairs. She whisked down the hall. The thick pile of the carpet swallowed all sound—and how kind it felt to her feet after the lumps and bumps outside! Suddenly, before she could notice it and stop herself, she was opposite another doorway. Her horror-stricken glance through the door revealed a breakfast tableau: Maggie with a coffee pot bending over Mrs. Walker; Cousin Jane's stout, rigid back; a side-view of Robert hunched over and sullenly staring into his lap.

Then she was past the door. None of them had noticed.

'Oh, what a piece of dumb luck!' she thought, clutching her hands to her head as she flew up the stairs. 'I can hide in Vicky's room till Bobbie comes up.'

Victoria's door was shut. Could she still be sleeping? Susan knocked softly. There was a stir on the other side of the door, and Victoria whispered, "Bobbie?"

"No," Susan whispered back, "it's—" and then there was the sound of heavy slow footsteps on the stairs.

"Bobbie?" Victoria whispered again.

Susan turned the knob and pushed. The door would not open. The footsteps were ascending . . . Her eyes darted about the hallway. There was an open door! She scurried through it, dropped to the floor, and rolled under the bed. She had a glimpse in passing of maps and flags and a sword on the wall—it must be Robert's room, thank goodness!

The heavy footsteps came down the hall and into the room. She could see Robert's shoes coming up to the bed. She heard him groan. His feet vanished and the springs creaked as he threw himself down.

"Bobbie!" she whispered, scrambling out.

The springs gave a violent creak. "Vick!" he whispered. "What're you—?" Then he saw who it was. "Great Caesar!" he croaked. His face went white.

"What's the matter?" she whispered. "It's me!"

"But you—we thought—" he stammered. He touched her face with an icy hand. "Did you get another trip back on the elevator?"

"We never went!"

"But you left your shoes and a letter in the hall!"

"Oh!" she cried, slapping her forehead. She'd forgotten that letter!

"Not so loud!" Robert jumped to the door and closed it. "Oh, Sue! We thought you'd gone for good. We thought the wishing well had failed. Vicky's been crying her eyes out."

"Oh, I *am* sorry! I thought it was all over, too, when I wrote that letter, and then something happened and I forgot to take the letter with me when we went back to the Hollisters'. Why is Vicky's door locked?"

Robert made a face. "Cousin Jane . . . She's locked Vick up and put her on short rations. She didn't know we were out of the house yesterday, but just after I got back she ambushed me and asked where Vicky was. I said I was sure she was in the house somewhere, and she went searching, and I had to throw my arrowheads and Vick's mirror out the window. And when poor Vick came back from the wishing well, Cousin Jane pounced on her and just blew her up. And then Mama tried to defend her, and oh my, what a row! The punishment could be worse, I guess. Cousin Jane doesn't know it, but the key to my door fits Vicky's door, and there's a key to one of the closets downstairs that fits both of them. Vick and I found that out long ago when we were playing Prisoner of Chillon. So it means I can keep her in victuals. If her appetite were only better she'd be eating as well as the rest of us. I found your letter and the shoes this morning, by the way, while I was on a foraging raid for her."

"Could I have the shoes back? My feet are killing me!"

"Totus dexter. They're in Vick's room. Hey, what *did* happen last night?"

Susan brought him up to date on the events of last night and this morning.

"So now," she concluded, "Daddy's thinking about what to do next, and he wants to talk to you."

"We'll go right now!" He jumped up, then exclaimed, "Oh, your shoes! Mmm . . . I know—we'll smuggle a communication in to the prisoner." He ran over to his desk, and scrawled a note:

> *Mr. Shaw and Sue still here!! Mr. Shaw's heart smitten at last!!! Sue needs shoes, please hand them out. Destroy this dispatch.*

"Totus dexter! Now . . ." He carefully opened his door

and beckoned Susan over. "You stand there," he whispered, "and keep a lookout down the stairs. Soon as you see or hear anything, give me a signal and retreat back here."

She nodded, and slipped over to the place he had pointed out. He crept to Victoria's door, knocked very quietly, and thrust the message underneath the door. There was a moment of silence, and then a muffled squeak from within. Robert unlocked the door, and Victoria's head popped out. She looked wild, with rumpled hair and tear-reddened eyes. Her mouth dropped open with unbelieving joy as she caught sight of Susan. Susan waved, trying to say with that gesture, "Oh, Vicky, it's finally really happened, and I don't know how we're going to do it, but we are!" "*Shoes!*" Robert pantomimed. Victoria vanished, and reappeared an instant later with the shoes. She blew a kiss at Susan. Robert closed the door and locked it, and he and Susan tiptoed swiftly back to his room.

She had no sooner stuffed her aching feet into the shoes when Robert murmured, "I think they're coming up, Sue. Quick! Back stairs!"

Footsteps were already sounding on the front stairway as they ran down the hall. Cousin Jane's voice crackled, "Isabelle, I would strongly suggest that you discharge Maggie as soon as you are in the city, if not sooner. People in reduced circumstances cannot afford—" and then Robert closed another door behind them, and they were in the darkness of the back staircase. These stairs were not carpeted, and their footsteps clattered and reverberated. Robert opened the door at the bottom, poked his head out, and called, "Maggie?"

"Sure and ye make enough clip-clap for two on them stairs!"

"Are you going to clear away the breakfast things now?"

"As soon as Herself's out o' the way, an' not before."

"She's upstairs with Mama now."

Maggie heaved a great sigh. "Ah, well . . . She's not after plaguin' us much longer, there's a comfort."

"What do you mean?"

Maggie's voice sank. "Didn't I have a dream last night, as clear as ever was? Herself is goin' on a long, long journey when she least expects it. You watch! An' good riddance!" Her voice faded out of the kitchen.

"Don't I wish it, too!" Robert muttered. "Come on, Sue—quiet through the kitchen, and then run like blazes!"

⋞ 16. MR. SHAW'S PLAN ⋟

> *. . . in much better spirits after thinking about things. He had a really marvellous idea for taking care of Mr. Sweeney and getting our treasure back. The only thing wrong with it is that it's going to happen in the dark, so I won't get to see Mr. Sweeney's face when we spring the trap . . .*

"Good, good, there you are!" Mr. Shaw cried when they burst into the stable. "I was beginning to wonder if you'd ever— How are you, Bobbie?"

"Corporal Walker reporting and ready for duty, sir!"

"At ease, Corporal," Mr. Shaw laughed. "I have some duty for you, all right. How is your mother? And Vicky?"

"Well . . . they're bearing up, sir."

Susan explained the situation in the Walker household to her father.

"By George!" Mr. Shaw said, clenching his fists. "I hate to say anything against a relative, Bobbie, but that—that cousin of yours really goes too far."

"Oh, I agree one hundred percent, sir! I think Mama's beginning to see through her, too. She pretends to be helping us, and maybe she is, a little; but it's mostly just an excuse for bullying us about."

"Well, she has no right to bully you about, and she *can't* bully me about, and when the time comes— Well, we'll deal with that later; right now we have other business. Did Susie tell you about Mr. Sweeney and his plans for us?"

"Yes, sir. Oh, I wish I were grown up! I'd give him such a thrashing!"

"Steady, steady! It's what he deserves, all right, but I've thought of something even better. Susie and I found a curious message in the elevator last night, and it's given me an idea." Mr. Shaw grinned and rubbed his hands. "Mr. Sweeney thinks he has plans for us, does he? Well, I have plans for *him*."

"Oh, Daddy, what?"

"Well, first I'm going to put a tail on him, as they say in detective stories."

Robert looked blank.

"Twentieth-century talk, Bobbie—it means I'm going to have him followed. Trailed. By you, if you're willing."

"Oh, absolutely, sir! What do you want me to find out?"

"All I want to know is where he's staying. He doesn't want me to know, so the chances are good that he's hiding the treasure there. You know the neighborhood, Bobbie. Where could he be living?"

"Well, there's the Knutsens and the Blalocks that way, and the Varnums and the Schultzes and the Besemers *that* way. He might be staying anywhere in town, for that matter."

"No, I think he'll stay away from town—he's been playing his dirty tricks there too, you know . . . Well, wherever it is, I know you'll find it. He's coming here for a progress report in a few hours. When he leaves, he's all yours."

"Totus dexter, sir! I know just where to wait for him, too—the old apple orchard."

"Daddy, I still don't know what you're up to."

"Simple, my dear. We learn where Sweeney is living; we arrange for his prolonged absence; and we reclaim what he took from us."

"There's more to it than that," she insisted. "I can tell by the way you're smiling."

"You're right, there is more. It's Mr. Sweeney's prolonged absence that tickles my fancy at the moment. I have decided that if I am going to live in this world, I don't want Sweeney in it. Therefore, I am going to remove him—permanently."

"Oh, but, sir—!" and "*Daddy*—!" Robert and Susan said simultaneously.

He gave a shout of laughter. "Oh, the looks on your faces! No, I don't mean anything *that* drastic. What I had in mind was something harmless, but absolutely final. I want to give him a present—the last trip from here on the elevator."

"Ah-h-h!" Susan cried, clasping her hands.

"Oh, sir, that's magnificent!"

"I'm kind of pleased with the idea myself," Mr. Shaw laughed. "It should be simple enough to do, too—we just have to lead him on in the right way. When he comes for his progress report, I'm going to tell him that you've made an impression of the key, Susie—that's the key to your mother's fictitious jewel box, Bobbie—and that I'm going to have a copy of the key made. I'm going to tell him that the Walkers have invited you to spend the night, Susie, and that you'll take the key and do the dirty work as soon as everyone's asleep. I'm going to tell him that all we have to do, he and I, is to sneak into the Walkers' house at midnight and collect the booty from you. So he *should* walk right up to the elevator with his tongue hanging out, the rat. And we'll just—oh, assist him into it, and send him on his way with a long farewell! But of course, we'll have to make preparations . . . Bobbie, will you see to it that the doors to your house are unlocked?"

"Trust me, sir!"

"Good. Now, Susie, what you're going to do is creep into the house as soon as everyone's settled down for the night. When is that usually, Bobbie?"

"About ten-thirty, sir."

"A little after ten-thirty then, chick. I don't think Sweeney will be spying on us at that time of night, but he will be coming to meet me about eleven-thirty, so I want you out of sight well before then. Now, you should have a pillowcase with something fairly heavy inside, to represent the jewels."

"That's easy—Vicky and I can fix that up. You'll have her door unlocked too, won't you, Bobbie?"

"Leave it to me, Sue."

"Now, at eleven-thirty," Mr. Shaw went on, "call up

the elevator, Susie. That's a lot earlier than we need it, but it's best to have everything ready beforehand. You'd better stick a wedge in the slot to keep the door open— you never know with that elevator when it's going to decide to close up again. Also, somebody down below might try to call it back, and we have to prevent that."

"What'll I use for a wedge?"

"Oh, a folded-up newspaper or magazine should do it. Bobbie, could you—?"

"Yes, sir. I'll have it all ready for her."

"Fine! Next step, Susie: turn out the light in the elevator. We'll want everything as dark as possible. If you can't find the switch, unscrew the lightbulb."

"All right. How do we 'assist' Mr. Sweeney into the elevator, Daddy?"

"That part will be up to me. He and I will come through the kitchen into the hallway. You'll be waiting in front of the open elevator with the pillowcase in your hands. Hold it out to the side, like this. When Sweeney puts out his slimy paws to take it, I will shove him into the elevator—hard enough, I hope, to take the wind out of his sails. The minute he goes in, chick, grab the wedge out of the door slot. I'll reach inside and press a button. And farewell, Mr. Sweeney!"

"Isn't there anything else that *I* can do, sir?"

"Yes. I think you and Victoria should be hiding behind the curtains in the hallway. I want you to be ready to come swarming out in case Sweeney needs more assistance than I can give him by myself."

"Oh, capital, sir! And in case he's going to be really troublesome, I'll have my cavalry saber—!"

"No!" Mr. Shaw said. "No. I'm sorry, Bobbie, but it's going to be dark, and there'll be too many of us bumping around in a small area to take chances with anything sharp. If he needs more persuasion, we'll apply it with our hands, and nobody'll get hurt."

"Isn't it going to be awfully noisy, Daddy?"

"That's the drawback," Mr. Shaw sighed. "Even at best there's going to be a pretty heavy thump . . . I hate the idea of alarming Mrs. Walker, and if Cousin Jane is aroused—!" He shook his head. "But I just don't know how we can avoid a certain amount of racket."

"I don't think a little noise will matter, sir. If Mama or Cousin Jane do come down to see what's happening, we'll hear them. You and Susan can retreat out the kitchen door before they get to the hallway, and Vicky and I'll sort of fade up the back stairs and return to our rooms, and the whole thing will be blamed on Toby."

"Poor Toby!" Susan laughed. "He *is* handy that way, though."

"Well, I suppose that'll be all right, then," Mr. Shaw said. "If it is blamed on Toby, I'll see that he gets something he likes. Now, the only other thing that worries me is Maggie—she could spoil the whole plan just by making an appearance at the wrong moment. Does she wander around a lot at night?"

Robert grinned. "Only to catch me, sir. But we have an understanding now. As long as Vicky's locked up, I'm foraging for *her,* and Maggie said she'd stay in her room and let me."

"Ah! Well, if that's the case, then, I don't see how we can fail."

"Oh, we won't fail, sir! Mr. Sweeney's doom is sealed!"

They went over the plan once more, to be certain that each knew what was going to be done by whom, and when. Robert was to explain everything to Victoria that evening, as soon as it was safe to release her from captivity.

"Now, Bobbie," Mr. Shaw concluded, "you said you were going to lie in wait for Sweeney in the apple orchard? Fine! I think maybe you'd better take your station there right now. It's long before he's due, of course, but . . . well, I don't want to take any chances. He might just happen to come early, or he might spy around here for a while before he makes his appearance."

"I understand, sir."

"And listen—I can't impress this on you too strongly: *don't let him see you.* He's threatened to denounce me to the police if he finds out he's being followed, and I think he means it. Not that we have anything to fear from the police, but as soon as he tells on us he'll take the treasure and decamp, and there'll go our last chance of ever getting it back. So *don't,* for heaven's sake, even let him suspect you're on his trail."

"I won't, sir—trust me."

"And when you know for certain where he's staying, come back and report to me. And tonight—" Mr. Shaw smiled and pointed downward. "And then with *that* behind us, we can begin to consider how to deal with Cousin Jane."

"Yes, sir. Confusion to the enemy!"

"Exactly. Well, goodbye and good luck, Corporal."

"Goodbye, Bobbie. Be careful!"

"Goodbye, sir. Goodbye, Sue. I will."

They all shook hands. Robert gave them a final salute, and vanished out the door.

. . . played his little scene with Mr.
Sweeney to perfection! We had to spend
the rest of the day waiting, and it was
awful. At least Daddy could go to town and
work off some of his nervous energy. I didn't
have anything to do but worry. And there
was plenty to worry about, such as the
police visiting the Walkers, and the fact that
Bobbie never came to make his report . . .

Mr. Sweeney gave a discreet cough. So quietly had he made his approach that Mr. Shaw, sitting on the sack of oats, yawning with nervousness and pretending to read a newspaper, never heard him. Susan had been caught napping, too—almost literally. She was in the loft, buried under some hay. The hay tickled her neck, but it was so warm that she had allowed her eyes to close.

The Shaws both jumped. Mr. Shaw lowered his paper, and Susan put her eye to a crack in the floorboards.

"Ah there, Shaw," Mr. Sweeney said in his smoothest tone. "Catching up with the wide world, I see."

"Yes, I, ah, thought I'd see what was happening." Mr. Shaw folded the paper, which happened to be two weeks old, and put it down.

"You did not pay your respects to Isabelle this morning?"

Mr. Shaw's jaw tightened. "Are you asking me, Sweeney, or telling me?"

Mr. Sweeney smiled. "My dear fellow, I keep my eye on what concerns me."

"All right, then, I did not visit Mrs. Walker this morning. Mrs. Walker believes that I am in town consulting with various gentlemen about the most profitable ways of investing the money she entrusted to me."

"How droll! Well, of course, *now* you can assure her that her fortune is in the best possible hands. Ah, ah, ah!—philosophy, my dear Shaw!"

Mr. Shaw glared and muttered something under his breath.

"Where is your gifted daughter?"

"Playing with the Walker children. Why?"

"Oh, I just found it curious that I didn't see her going there."

Mr. Shaw shrugged. "The children have their own ways of going and coming. Susan, as a matter of fact, has been to the Walkers' for more amateur theatricals, and has been in touch with me since. The results have been gratifying."

He pulled from his pocket and held out for inspection two lumps of beeswax which he had obtained from Mrs. Hollister. Impressed in them was the outline of a little key that he had found in a bowl of buttons, pins and other oddments on the chest of drawers in his room.

Mr. Sweeney shook his head in admiration. "That girl is—an—Artist!" he declared.

"Yes. I'll just stroll into town this afternoon and have a key made from this. Susan will find the key with her nightgown and robe and toothbrush when she comes to fetch them later in the day. You see, she's managed to secure an invitation to spend the night at the Walkers'."

"Ah!" Mr. Sweeney breathed.

"So the rest of the operation should be absurdly simple. Why don't you meet me here at midnight? We can proceed to the Walkers' house, and enter through the

144

kitchen door—Susan will make sure it's unlocked for us. She will meet us inside, where she will hand over to us a cloth bag—a heavily-laden cloth bag." Mr. Shaw leered at this point so realistically that Susan could hardly suppress a giggle. "She will return to bed, while you and I go somewhere to divide the, ah, take. After that, I sincerely hope to say goodbye to you forever."

Mr. Sweeney rubbed his hands. "An excellent plan, Shaw. However, certain amendments will be necessary. For one thing, you and I will not by any means say farewell after our division of the spoils."

"Why not, for heaven's sake?"

"Oh, don't be tiresome, Shaw! I assure you it's not because I enjoy your company any more than you enjoy mine. But I know enough to watch out for my own interests. Why should I assume, as you obviously wish me to, that the bag is going to have the whole take in it? *I* know that Susan is cool enough to walk out of the Walkers' house tomorrow morning—right under Isabelle's nose, too!—with her overnight case bulging with booty that she somehow 'forgot' to put in the cloth bag. Obviously I can't say any farewells until she has reported back to you *in my presence.*"

"You intend to search my daughter's effects, sir?"

"Of course."

"Damn you for a scoundrel!" Mr. Shaw roared, stamping his foot.

'Well done, Daddy!' Susan thought. 'You're playing this scene like a real pro!'

"Philosophy!" Mr. Sweeney laughed. "My concern is only to remove temptations from your path, Shaw! Now, I must insist on another change. We will meet in the Walkers' stable, not here."

"All right—but may I ask why?"

145

Mr. Sweeney looked at Mr. Shaw with unfeigned puzzlement. "*Why?* Shaw, sometimes you baffle me. The reason is, of course, that tonight there will be a horse in this stable, whose noise might betray our presence, whereas the Walkers' stable will be empty."

"Oh. Yes . . ." Mr. Shaw rubbed his face, and continued with a sigh, "I keep forgetting these little details."

Mr. Sweeney gave a superior smile. "Shaw, in this game there is nothing *but* detail. Now, one more amendment, and I'll have done. We will meet in the Walkers' stable at sundown, not at midnight. I want to keep my eye on you, frankly. There are just too many hours of darkness before midnight, during which you and Susan could—oh, succumb to temptation, shall we say? Sundown, then?"

Mr. Shaw pretended reluctance, but finally growled, "All right."

"Excellent. Just bear in mind that you have everything to lose if you cross me in the least particular. Have you anything more to say to me?"

"Nothing that you'd want to hear, Sweeney."

"Philosophy, Shaw! Next to a scrupulous attention to detail, that is the greatest asset we have in our profession. Good day, then—until sundown!"

Mr. Shaw strode to the door and watched him angle across the pasture. "Come on down, chick!" he said quietly. She scrambled out from under the hay, and half climbed, half slid down the ladder from the loft. "Hold it, hold it," he muttered. "Not yet . . . All right, he's over the ridge. Run!"

They dashed for the Hollisters' back door.

"Our fish," he said when they were inside, "seems to have swallowed the bait."

"Daddy, you were marvelous!"

She got the giggles as they went upstairs. As soon as they were in his room she declaimed, "Are you going to search my daughter's effects, sir?" and fell into a chair, helpless with laughter.

Mr. Shaw grinned. "It did go off pretty well, didn't it? All except that part about forgetting Hollister's horse. Well, that's all right—the more superior he feels, the more relaxed he'll be. The unctuous creep! Well, it's Bobbie's show now. All we can do is wait."

"I *hate* waiting."

"Don't blame you. Oh! I guess I have to keep up the masquerade and go to town to have a key made. It'll be a nice walk, anyway."

"I can't go for a walk or anything, can I?"

"No! You sit tight—Weaselface might be watching."

She groaned.

In a little while he left. She brought her diary up to date, putting in plenty of detail in order to pass the time. The afternoon grew hotter as it wore on. She paced her room. She threw herself on the bed and tried to nap. She picked up a copy of *Harper's Bazar* ('Is that the way it's spelled?' she wondered), and leafed through it. "Paris Fashions," she read. "[From our own correspondent] It may be affirmed that the article most worn in Paris is fur. This fashion is imposed by the severe winter which we are undergoing . . ." Winter? She turned to the cover and looked at the date: February 7, 1880. Oh, foo! She dropped the magazine and began pacing again.

Mrs. Hollister scuffled and made mousey housekeeping sounds below. Flies buzzed against the window . . .

Mr. Shaw came back at four o'clock.

"Hello, chick! How're you doing? Did Bobbie show up yet?"

"No. Oh, what a beautiful hat!"

"Had to get it," he said, taking off a shiny new straw hat with a black ribbon, and mopping his brow. "Everybody was giving me funny looks. Bare heads are definitely out of style this year. Well, I hope Sweeney is watching—he can now conclude that we have a key to Mrs. Walker's jewel box."

He sat down with a sigh by the front window, and they had the waiting fidgets together.

⊰⊰⊰⊱⊱⊱

At five after five Mr. Shaw gave a start and said, "Oh oh! There's Maggie out in the road. She's got a bonnet on. Walking fast. Looks like she's going to town. Maybe they gave her the evening off."

"Or else she's been fired by Cousin Jane," Susan groaned.

There was another hour of waiting and fidgets, and muttering by Mr. Shaw over Robert's failure to report.

They heard the sound of hooves and wheels on the road. "Here comes Uncle Sam Windbag," Mr. Shaw sighed. He glanced out the window. "Oh oh! No it isn't. It's—a policeman, by George! Badge on his hat, anyway. With Maggie. I wonder what . . . Oh—good—*night!* Sweeney's done it!"

Susan's heart constricted. "You mean he—?"

"He must have caught Bobbie trailing him, and suspected we were behind it, and so he's told the police.— There they go, into the Walkers'. Oh, the dirty dog! There goes our fortune . . ."

"Wait, Daddy!—Maggie went out a while ago, and now she's come back with a policeman. It looks like the Walkers sent her to get one. Mr. Sweeney might not have anything to do with it!"

"Oh, lord!" he groaned. "I guess I'll have to go find out for sure."

When at last the policeman could be seen coming out of the Walkers' house and climbing into his buggy, Mr. Shaw ran out to intercept him. Susan peeked through the curtains and watched with a pounding heart. The policeman—he wore a derby!—pointed over his shoulder with his thumb at the Walkers' house. Mr. Shaw nodded. The policeman leaned forward. Mr. Shaw shook his head. They exchanged a few more words; then each raised a hand in farewell, and the buggy moved off down the road. Mr. Shaw came hurrying back to the house. He had no sooner gotten inside when Mr. Hollister's buggy appeared.

"Almost got caught by Uncle Sam!" he panted, bursting into the room and banging the door shut. "Phew! Narrow escape from a fate worse than death! Well, the fuss over at the Walkers' is that they think Bobbie's run away! That's Cousin Jane's conclusion, anyway. The policeman thinks she's called him into it just to create the maximum pain for everybody. He's probably right. He had a few words to say about her that express *my* sentiments exactly."

"Where do you think Bobbie is?—still trailing Mr. Sweeney?"

"He must be . . ." Mr. Shaw rubbed his chin for a minute. "You know, what's probably happening is that Sweeney is over there somewhere spying on us, and Bobbie is over there somewhere spying on *him,* and—oh, good night! You know what that means? It means Sweeney probably saw me out there talking to that cop!" He slapped his forehead. "What's he going to conclude from *that*? It might just make him nervous enough to run!"

Susan didn't know what to say. She chewed her knuckle and resumed her pacing.

Their dinner came up a short time later—Mr. Shaw was "indisposed" again—but they had little appetite for it. Mr. Hollister brayed below. Mrs. Hollister murmured. A group of birds had hysterics outside, presumably over Toby. The light turned golden, and then ruddy. The Shaws waited.

Robert did not come to make his report.

And then at last it was sundown. Mr. Hollister was delivering a monologue to his wife out on the veranda; his nasal bray went on and on without interruption, like a waterfall. Mr. Shaw stood up with a great sigh.

"All right, chick—it's time for me to go. If Sweeney doesn't show up soon, it means he's gone for good—with our fortune. In that case, I'll be back within an hour. If he does show up, we'll go through with everything as planned. I guess you and I can bring it off by ourselves, can't we? Just be sure to take a loaded pillowcase and a newspaper with you. Here, take my watch, too. If I don't come back, go to the Walkers' about eleven. Use the front door—the back door can be seen from the stable. Are you all straight now on what you're going to do over there?"

"Yes." An anxiety that had been building up in her for hours finally burst forth. "Daddy, what if something has happened to Bobbie?"

"Oh, hon, he probably just forgot that he was supposed to come make a report."

'But what if something *has* happened to him?"

"We'll go looking for him as soon as we're free. All right?"

She had to be satisfied with that.

He hugged her. "Goodbye, chick. Slow and easy, now.

It's all going to turn out fine."

She couldn't bring herself to say anything. They blew a kiss at each other, and Mr. Shaw slipped out, leaving her to wait alone.

18. MR. HOLLISTER
◦⟨ DEFENDS THE WIDOW'S HEARTH ⟩◦

> . . . *awful night! About the only thing that went right was that I got out of the house safely. I was worried sick about Bobbie. I waited in the back yard and then in the hedge until after eleven and went to the Walkers'. Everything began to get out of control . . .*

Mr. Shaw did not return. Mr. Sweeney must still be in the picture, then, and the plan would proceed.

It was a warm night with a nearly full moon alternately shining and hiding behind clouds. From the veranda came the creak of rocking chairs and Mr. Hollister's everlasting bray. She glanced at the watch again: only a few minutes until ten. 'They're *never* going to turn in!' she thought, chewing her knuckle. But it suddenly came to her that she didn't have to wait until the Hollisters were safely snoring in bed—she could go now. She could walk out the back door and sit under a bush or something until it was time to go to the Walkers'.

It was done in a minute. She slipped the watch into her pocket, blew out the candle, and crept out of the house. She carried a rolled-up copy of *Harper's Bazar* to jam the elevator door, and a pillowcase weighted with all the small heavy objects she could find.

The hedge would be the best place to wait, but she couldn't get to that part with the hole in it without the risk of being seen by the Hollisters. She decided to wait in the back yard for the time being, and made herself comfortable under a small tree.

As comfortable as she could, that is, considering her state of mind. What had happened to Bobbie? Could he have just *forgotten* about coming to report to them? That didn't sound like Corporal Robert Lincoln Walker. Was he injured or stuck somewhere out in the fields or woods? Her heart failed her.

Some time later Mr. Hollister's voice ceased braying and turned into a huge yawn. Mrs. Hollister's voice murmured something. "N-yas, n-yas," Mr. Hollister trumpeted. There was a sound of footsteps on loose floorboards, and protesting door-hinges.

Susan jumped up and slipped across the yard to the hedge. A light went out on the third floor of the Walkers' house. 'Well, there's one of them down, anyway,' she thought. She peered at the greenish glow of the watch hands: ten-thirty-five. "Go to bed, please!" she hissed at the house. There was still a faint glow of light in the downstairs windows . . .

She waited.

The glow vanished from the downstairs windows and reappeared in two of the upstairs windows in the back of the house.

She waited.

Ah! There went the upstairs light. She looked at the

time: ten to eleven. She would wait until a quarter after.

She waited for twenty-five minutes, and then for a few more to allow the moon to go behind a cloud.

Now she could go! She scurried across the yard to the front porch, slipped off her shoes, and padded up to the door.

It was locked.

'Oh, good grief!' she thought wearily. Robert was supposed to have taken care of the doors. If they were still locked, it meant that he—oh, she couldn't worry about that now! She crept down the steps and put her shoes back on. She'd have to try the kitchen door. And if *it* was locked—? Well, check first and ask questions later . . .

But no—she *couldn't* try the back door. Her father had told her not to, because it was visible from the stable . . .

Windows, then—how about windows?

Back on the porch she went, and crept up to the window closest to the door.

What was that?

She froze and listened. Out on the road there was the faint rhythmic sound of hooves and wheels. Her instinct was to slip away from the porch and hide. But no—the road was far from the house, the porch was in shadow —no one would notice her. She turned back to the window and pushed up on its unyielding frame.

The hooves clopped, the iron-rimmed wheels crunched on the gravel, past the Hollisters', past the hedge, past the—no, *not* past the Walkers'. The sounds stopped at the front gate. The horse gave a flubbery snort and shook its harness. There were voices. There were lights. "Oh, no!" Susan gasped. Dark figures with bull's-eye lanterns were coming up the walk.

She scurried to the end of the porch, threw her leg over the railing, and slid down into the hydrangeas.

A rumbling voice said, "All right, young-feller-me-lad, *now* we'll see."

"Why'ncha lea'me alone?" a boy's voice whined. "I never been here in my life."

"Dunno, Frank," another man's voice said. "I don't think he's the one. Lady distinctly told me brown hair. This kid—"

"She wants a runaway," Frank rumbled, "and we *got* a runaway. Up to her to say if he's the one or not."

"I ain't no runaway. I was just goin' to visit my Cousin Florrie. Lea'me alone."

Boots clomped up the steps and across the porch. Circles of light darted about. There was a thunderous knocking at the door.

"She a reg'lar fierce 'un, Frank. I wish you'd—"

"Dooty is dooty," Frank rumbled. "She reported a run-away, and we—"

The house echoed to a renewed application of the knocker. Then came the sound of the bolt being hurled back, and the door opened with a crash.

"What is the meaning of this?" Cousin Jane snapped.

"Police, ma'am. We—"

"What is it—what is it?" Mrs. Walker's voice cried from within.

"Go back to bed, Isabelle. I will deal with this."

"You're looking for a runaway boy, I believe."

"I am not. *You* were supposed to be looking for him, but he has returned. Who is this? You were not seriously going to present *this* vagabond as a candidate, were you?"

"Ma'am, you reported a runaway boy. We had a run-away boy. We—"

"No one with half an eye in his head could possibly imagine that *this* grimy little heathen could belong to this house. You are bunglers, sir! I shall lodge a complaint with your superiors in the morning. Good night to you."

The door shut with a crash that set the glass a-rattle, and the bolt snapped home like a rifle-shot.

"Told you, Frank," said an apologetic murmur. "We should've—"

"Well, melt—my—badge—for—a—revolving—rat-trap!" Frank rumbled on a rising note. "All right, my high and mighty hoity-toity Duchess, just you—"

"Ow!" the boy yelped. "Leggo my ear!"

"—just you come crying to us again with your run-aways, or your arson, or your robbery—" their boots thumped down the steps, down the walk "—or your bloody *murder* even, and see if I don't show you the broad side of my—" His voice went on indistinctly through the gate. The buggy creaked. "Gee yup!" he roared. His whip cracked, and the horse went cantering down the lane with the sound of a massed cavalry charge.

'Well,' Susan sighed to herself, 'at least Bobbie's safe . . . *Why* didn't he ever come to tell us what he found out? Good grief, it'll take everybody forever to settle down in the house now . . . Wonder if Daddy and Mr. Sweeney heard all that?' She looked at the watch: three minutes till midnight! Her stomach flopped over at a new thought. What if the two men had *not* heard the disturbance? The whole house had been between them and it, after all . . . In that case, they would be coming to the back door in a few minutes! And here she was, still outside . . .

There was no more time for caution. She scrambled back on the porch through the clutching branches of hydrangea, and leaped to the window. The lower sash would not go up. Maybe the upper sash would come down? No. Next window, then. She pushed and panted at its sashes without result.

"*Stop, thieves!*" a voice shouted from the Hollisters' house. Susan gave a start that lifted her feet clear off the porch floor.

"*Horse thieves!*" Mr. Hollister bawled. "*Cutthroats! Don't move—I've got you in my sights, you Republican sneaks!*"

An instant of silence, then: 'Oh, you will, will you?"

BALOOM! said a very large gun. Echoes bounced between the two houses and their stables: *whap whap whap whap whap* . . .

The echoes died away into a dreadful waiting quiet. Susan cowered in terror.

A door slammed at the Hollisters'. Footsteps pounded down the Hollisters' walk, on the road, through the Walkers' gate. The moon revealed Mr. Hollister, dressed in boots and white nightshirt, and carrying a gun nearly as long as himself.

Once more Susan threw her leg over the railing, and dropped down into the hydrangeas.

Mr. Hollister thumped up on the porch, pounded the door, and waited, breathing heavily and muttering "N-yas, n-yas," to himself.

The door crashed open, and Cousin Jane shouted, "Are we to have no peace tonight?"

"N-yas, ma'am!" Mr. Hollister brayed. "I believe the customary tranquillity of our rural—ha—nocturne has been restored. Hiram W. Hollister at your service, ma'am. I—"

"This is an outrage!" Cousin Jane cried.

"It is indeed, ma'am!" Mr. Hollister trumpeted. "I share and endorse your sense of abomination! Perilous times, ma'am! But for my alertness and quick action, you and yours might have been murdered in your very beds, ma'am!"

"What?"

Mr. Hollister's voice sank four tones. "Night prowlers, ma'am. I was awakened from my peaceful slumbers by the sound of their horses and vehicles. Looking out my window, I espied a gang of them creeping out of your stable and toward your house with sinister intent. I did not falter, ma'am! I addressed them in no uncertain terms, and fired a warning shot over their heads. My resolution took the heart out of 'em, ma'am! They have dispersed, and I believe I can safely say that our accustomed—ha—serenity reigns supreme."

"Well, sir, I suppose we must thank you," Cousin Jane

said grudgingly. "You will be suitably rewarded in the morning."

"Oh, no, ma'am!" Mr. Hollister brayed. "With all respect, allow me to tender my refusal. The knowledge that I have successfully defended a widow's hearth and home, ma'am, is reward enough for—"

"Very well, sir. Thank you and good night. Pray do not raise your voice or discharge your weapon again. I assure you that this house is securely locked. If any ruffian manages to gain entrance notwithstanding, I shall make him regret it. Good night, sir."

The door closed smartly, the bolt clicked into place, and Mr. Hollister stumped away, muttering "N-yas, n-yas," as he went.

Susan chewed on her knuckle and pondered her next move. What were her father and Mr. Sweeney going to do now? How far had they been "dispersed" by Mr. Hollister? Would they give up, or would they wait and try to enter the house when all was calm again? 'Oh, good grief!' she thought. 'I guess I'd better try to find out what they're up to. If I stick close to the bushes, I might be able to get a look at them that'll tell me something. *If* they're still back there . . .'

She crawled out from under the hydrangeas, and began to creep around the right side of the house—the side away from the Hollisters'. There were two bays jutting out on this side. She had just reached the second one when she heard a stealthy sliding sound over her head.

⊰ 19. CORPORAL WALKER'S ORDEAL ⊱

*. . . have to go back and tell what
happened to Bobbie first. When we were
comparing stories later he said he almost
ruined his special mission right at the
beginning. The rest of what went wrong
wasn't really his fault . . .*

Robert's lying-in-wait station was a gnarled Northern
Spy on the edge of the orchard. Sitting with his back
against its trunk, he could just see the Hollisters' stable
through a waving screen of grass. He raised his face to
the sunlight, closed his eyes, and thought about the day
ahead.

There would be a row with Cousin Jane when he got
back, of course. She would probably want to lock him up
in his room. He would have to put his key in his shoe
before he returned home, so that when she asked for it
he could say that he had lost it, turning his pockets out
for verification. Then if she did manage to lock him up
anyway, he could still escape, and let Vicky out, and
have everything ready for the execution of the plan.

As for the plan itself, he considered it brilliant. If
there was any flaw at all, it was that he, Corporal
Walker, would not be able to bring his cavalry saber into
the action. It would really be capital if only—if only
. . . A scene began to take shape in his mind: Mr. Shaw
lay on the parquet floor, unconscious through some mishap; Susan and Victoria cowered in the shadows, wide-
eyed with admiration; Mr. Sweeney, snarling with rage,
backed into the elevator, quailing under the fearless

frown of Corporal Walker. Blood trickled from a picturesque wound on Corporal Walker's forehead, and the razor-keen blade of his saber gleamed . . .

He awoke with a start, just in time to see Mr. Sweeney in the flesh disappearing over the ridge in Hollisters' pasture.

"Great Caesar!" he sobbed. He leaped up and dashed toward the pasture, pommeling his head with both fists. Two more seconds of slumber, and his special mission would have failed utterly . . . He demoted himself to Private on the spot. 'One more little mistake like that, Private, and I will drum you out of the regiment altogether!' he raged.

He popped over the ridge in the pasture too quickly. 'Look out, you idiot!' his mind shouted. Mr. Sweeney was halfway to the woodlot, but had paused and was turning around. Robert dove into the grass. 'Oh, look here, Private!' he roared inside. 'This won't do *at all!* Going too fast is just as bad as falling asleep. What kind of a scout *are* you?' If there had been a rank lower than Private, he would have demoted himself to it immediately.

After a while he raised his head very slowly. Mr. Sweeney was striding into the elephant-grey beeches and shaggy hickories of the woodlot. Robert slunk after him at a half-crouch, ready to drop instantly. His heart was beating high, but his head was steady now.

Mr. Sweeney led him through the woodlot, slantwise down the next meadow, across Ward Lane, and then behind the Ward Lane hedgerow until he came to a place opposite the Walker and Hollister homesteads. Here, in a thicket of sumac and elderberry, he could watch the houses without being seen from them. He sat down and made himself comfortable with his back against a boulder. Robert crept up as closely as he dared, ending under a clump of hawthorns about fifty feet behind and to the left of Mr. Sweeney. He carefully stretched himself out, rested his chin in his hands, and watched.

It slowly, painfully, maddeningly became clear that Mr. Sweeney intended to sit there for the rest of the afternoon, with only an occasional recess behind a willow thicket to take a few quick puffs on his cigar. Robert sweated in the heat, and shifted his weight, and blew at the wasps and bees and flies that hovered in front of his face, and crushed the spiders and other fauna that wandered into his sleeves and down his collar, and stifled the sneezes that bulged in his nose, and tried to ignore the hunger pangs that pinched his stomach with growing insistence, and shed tears of vexation, and yawned, and fought against the desire to lower his head and close his eyes for just a minute, and bit his lip, and lectured himself on the duty of a scout . . . and endured.

Only a few events punctuated the endless afternoon. Mrs. Hollister came out on her veranda and flapped her dustrag. Maggie appeared with a bucket and mop to sluice down the Walkers' front porch. Mr. Shaw came walking back from town in a new straw hat. Mr. Sweeney made an ironical salute toward his back as he went up the Hollisters' walk. Maggie set off townward in her bonnet. That was strange, Robert thought; it seemed too late in the afternoon for her to go strolling . . . A buggy came from town with—great Caesar!—a policeman and Maggie in it; they went into the Walkers'. Mr. Sweeney became as tense as a watchspring, and a sick anxious fear crept through Robert's heart. What was the matter at home, what could have happened? Ah, here came the policeman again, alone. And here came Mr. Shaw out

161

of Hollisters' to talk to him. Mr. Sweeney's back went rigid. Then the policeman drove on, Mr. Shaw ran back into the house, Mr. Hollister drove into his stable, and all was calm again—except Robert's wildly speculating mind.

Mr. Sweeney retreated behind the willows and smoked the remainder of his cigar in quick, short puffs. Obviously his mind was in a turmoil of speculation, too.

But he calmed down again, returned to his watching place, and kept a lookout for another hour. Then he got up and went behind the willows for—no! He was walking away.

'Ah!' Robert thought. '*Now* we'll find out what we want to know.' It was dinnertime—as the painful state of his own interior told him—and Mr. Sweeney must be going to his lodgings to fortify himself for the night's villainy. Robert heaved himself up, clenched his teeth against the pain in his stiff joints and muscles, and began to stalk his quarry.

But Mr. Sweeney did not go to the Knutsens', or the Blalocks', or anywhere else that Robert had mentioned to Mr. Shaw. He went by devious ways to the great beech woods that crowned the hill some three-quarters of a mile distant from the two houses, and plunged in. Presently he could be heard breaking sticks.

Robert crept with exquisite care between the trees to the edge of a small glade. There was Mr. Sweeney in his shirtsleeves, crouched in front of an improvised stone fireplace, touching a match flame to a small heap of sticks. His coat and hat were hung on a nearby snag; underneath, a blanket was spread out on a pile of dead leaves; and beside this bed, lined up with mathematical exactness, were a calfskin valise, a box of cigars, an extra pair of boots, and shaving tackle.

'A camp!' Robert thought. Of course—it made more sense than lodging with people who might snoop or ask questions . . . Suddenly he had an idea. Mr. Sweeney would surely want to gloat over the purloined treasure before the light failed. Why not watch until that happened? *Wouldn't* it be a triumph to report to Mr. Shaw that he had discovered the exact place where Mr. Sweeney had hidden it! Above and beyond the call of duty . . .

He hugged himself, and settled down to watch.

There followed a very bad half-hour, during which Mr. Sweeney slowly and fastidiously dined on toasted muffins and cheese, and drank tea. 'Ah, you scoundrel!' Robert thought, while his mouth watered and his stomach rumbled. 'Well, enjoy it while you can, you villain—it's your last dinner in this century.'

'Now!' he told himself when Mr. Sweeney had finished. But Mr. Sweeney was not in a gloating mood yet. He laid himself down on his blanket, and luxuriated in a cigar. Then for a long time he did nothing. Then he smoked another cigar.

'Oh, thunderation, come *on!*' Robert groaned. Daylight was beginning to dim . . .

Ah! Now! For Mr. Sweeney suddenly started out of his reverie, glanced skyward, and jumped up. He threw his cigar butt into the embers, put on his coat and hat, slipped something from the valise into his coat pocket, and strode away—passing so close to where Robert lay hidden that Robert could have touched him.

Now what? Robert followed with a rapidly beating heart.

Mr. Sweeney led him, in the gathering darkness, across fields and meadows, over fences, through hedgerows, across Ward Lane—and to the Walkers' own stable!

Robert's head whirled with puzzlement. He crept up to the side of the stable. Voices were murmuring inside. He laid his ear against the weathered boards. Mr. Sweeney and Mr. Shaw were talking inside.

They were speaking in such low voices that he couldn't hear what they were saying. He crept to the shelter of a mock orange bush where he could see the stable door, and crouched. Several windows in his house were lighted. It occurred to him for the first time—his heart gave a guilty lurch—that his mother might be seriously alarmed about his absence by now. He'd been gone almost the whole day . . . He'd better get back. But he was supposed to report to Mr. Shaw. How could he if—?

He waited, tense with anxiety, for more than an hour. Neither Mr. Shaw nor Mr. Sweeney reappeared. Well, he couldn't make his report, then. He *had* to go back and get the scene with Cousin Jane over with, so that everyone could calm down and go to bed. They simply had to be asleep before he could let Vicky out, and bring her up to date, and make everything ready to carry out the plan.

He sighed, and stood up. So much time wasted for nothing . . . !

≼ ≼ ≼ ≽ ≽ ≽

"I insist on knowing where you have been!" Cousin Jane snapped.

"Oh, Bobbie, Bobbie!" Mrs. Walker sobbed.

Her haggard, tear-stained face cut him to the center of his soul. "I can't tell you now, Mama," he wept. "All I can say is, it was all for the best. You'll see."

"For the *best!*" Cousin Jane snorted. "You were expressly forbidden to leave this house, and yet you have been gone for twelve hours. We have been sick with worry. We have been put to the trouble of calling in the police. Do you say that is for the *best*? What have you been up to?"

He shrank under the glitter of her eyes, but remained silent.

"You've been associating again with that Shaw girl, haven't you? With the daughter of a scoundrel, whom I forbade you ever to see again!"

"Bobbie," his mother wept.

"I'm sorry, Mama. Please believe me."

"Very well," Cousin Jane snapped. "We shall see about leaving this house 'all for the best.' Where is the key to your room, sir?"

"I—I lost it," he mumbled. It suddenly came to him that he had never put the key in his shoe after all. What if Cousin Jane demanded that he turn out his pockets—? He forced his hands to hang slack.

"*Lost* it? Have you no respect for anything? Very well, we shall see if this key fits." She took from her neck the string loop on which Victoria's key dangled, and pointed toward the stairs. "March!" she snapped.

"No," Mrs. Walker said.

Cousin Jane turned. "I beg your pardon, Isabelle?"

"I said, no!"

"You said *what*, Isabelle?"

"You are turning my house into a prison!" Mrs. Walker cried. "You lock all the doors. You have locked up my daughter. You are threatening to lock up my son. Why don't you lock Maggie up? Why not lock me up, too? Oh, you are a monster! I won't have it, I won't have it!"

"You wrote to me, Isabelle," Cousin Jane said in a

deadly calm voice. "You urgently requested my advice and my aid. You knew that I could not be spared from my duties with the Tropical Islands Civilizing Mission, and the United Gentlewomen's Crusade for the Suppression of Infamous Literature, and the Lady's Society for the Moral Instruction of the Laboring Classes. And yet you called on me; and I, without hesitation, hastened to your side. And what did I find, Isabelle? I found you keeping a sullen, hysterical and incompetent servant. I found your finances in total collapse. I found you entertaining—and *in the morning!*—an obvious scoundrel, a *man!* I found your children disrespectful and disobedient. But did I shrink? No. I have stood by you unflinchingly. I have tried to make your servant see her duty. I have attempted to order your affairs. I have patiently endeavored to guide your children's footsteps back to the path of civilized behavior. And at every step, Isabelle—" Cousin Jane's voice had been getting louder and louder, and was now crackling like a fusillade "—at every *turn*, Isabelle, you oppose me; argue with me; try to thwart me! IS THIS GRATITUDE?"

Mrs. Walker was weeping too wildly to answer. Robert felt such a desire to hurl himself headfirst into Cousin Jane's stomach that he almost swooned. 'Steady!' he heard a voice commanding him through the buzzing in his ears. 'The plan must proceed!'

"I—I am ready to accept—my punishment, ma'am," he choked.

"Come up!" she snapped, heading for the stairs. "In deference to your mother's demoralized state, I shall release you and your sister in the morning. But if you try to take advantage of my clemency in any way, you will regret it for a long time to come."

She marched him upstairs, holding a candle in one

hand and the key in the other. She tried the key in his door, and gave a little grunt of satisfaction on finding that it worked. She gestured him in with a nod, and snapped, "You will bring your sorrowing mother untimely to her grave, young man. Mend your ways, sir!" The door closed behind him, the key turned with a click, and he was alone in the dark.

He was shaking, but his heart was jubilant. 'Not bad,' he thought, 'not bad! You carried out your mission without getting caught, and you held firm in the face of the enemy.' He patted himself on the upper arm, restoring himself to rank. 'Not bad at all, *Corporal!*'

"Bedtime, Isabelle!" Cousin Jane commanded from the head of the stairs. "Your nerves are overwrought, and I am feeling somewhat fatigued myself. We must restore ourselves for the tasks of tomorrow."

All would be quiet soon. He would unlock his door, creep into Vick's room, tell her about the plan of campaign—

His hand froze for an instant, then clutched wildly in his pocket. A hot flash surged through his body. There was a hole in the bottom of his pocket, and the key was gone.

He collapsed on the bed, sobbing. In his mind's eye he tore the Corporal's stripes from his sleeve, snatched the decorations from his breast and trampled them underfoot, snapped his sword in half, and drummed himself out of the regiment forever.

◄ 20. THE PLAN IN RUINS ►

> . . . *from bad to worse. Our "cat fight"*
> *saved us and we got into the house finally,*
> *but I couldn't go to the elevator because*
> *Maggie came downstairs to fill her pitcher.*
> *Bobbie set Vicky free, but they were*
> *surprised by Cousin Jane. Bobbie got away.*
> *Everybody ended up downstairs. I was*
> *found by Cousin Jane. I knew it was all*
> *over when I saw Daddy and Mr. Sweeney*
> *come in . . .*

Susan shrank into the bushes and looked up. A second-story window was being opened, inch by inch . . .

Whose?

In her mind's eye she surveyed the inside of the house. When you went up the stairs, Vicky's room was here, Bobbie's was here; which meant, from the outside of the house, that—that she was now crouching under Bobbie's bay window.

Ch . . . ch . . . ch . . . Bit by bit the window sash slid up, until there was a gap of nearly two feet between it and the sill. For a few minutes Susan thought she could hear rustling sounds. These were followed by a quiet thump. A white shape materialized over the sill, and slithered groundward in a series of little jerks. It was a knotted bedsheet. Another thump . . . Out of the window came a pair of legs. The legs kicked. Then there was a gasp, a scrape of buttons over wood, and the rest of Robert appeared with a rush. His feet thunked against the carved wooden arch of a downstairs window.

'Good grief!' Susan thought. 'He'll put his foot through the glass in a minute! She must stop his swinging. She squeezed into the shrubbery, grabbed the end of the sheet, and pulled it to one side. His startled white face looked down on her over his arm.

"Bobbie!" she whispered. "It's—"

There was a ripping noise.

He gave a stifled yelp. The sheet went slack in her hands. She tried to throw herself aside, but it was too late. His weight struck her right shoulder, and they toppled into the shrubbery. The crash was like a forest tree collapsing.

She spat out a mouthful of leaves and twigs, and whispered, "You all right?"

"Think so. My ear hurts."

High above them came the sound of a window being thrown open.

"Cat fight!" Susan whispered. "Quick!" She rounded her lips and crooned, "Ow-w-w-w-w-w-w-w."

Robert caught on at once. "Oooo-oooo-oooo-oooo," he sang, *glissando*.

"Yow-wow-*wow!*" Susan shrieked, thrashing in the shrubbery with her legs.

Maggie's voice floated down through the darkness. "Wisha! Wisha! Get on out o' that, ye divels!" Something heavy clunked against her windowsill, and a stream of water cascaded down into the bush next to them.

"There's more o' that if ye want it," Maggie threatened. "And divel a drap o' milk will ye be gettin' from *me* in the mornin', Toby! Ye black limb o' Satan!"

The window slammed shut.

Susan let out a tremulous breath, and whispered, "Where've you *been*? Why were you climbing out the window?"

169

"Oh, Sue, I made such a mess of everything! Cousin Jane locked me up and then I found that I'd lost my key. What're you doing here?"

"I can't get in! Oh, it's all so awful—the whole plan is falling apart!"

"There's still a chance to make it work, Sue! Your Papa and Mr. Sweeney are hiding in the back yard! I saw them for a second over by the pond after Mr. Hollister fired. I'll bet they mean to carry on as soon as everything calms down again. We have to get ready for them!"

"How? We're locked out!"

"Nil desperandum, Sue. There's more than one way to get into the house. Come on!"

They extricated themselves from the wreckage of the shrubbery, and crept around to the other side of the house.

"Here," Robert whispered. "There's a broken pane in the cellar window. I can reach through and undo the catch." He dropped to his hands and knees to crawl under the hydrangeas. She crouched to follow him, but he whispered, "This is a hard way in, Sue. Go to the front door. I'll have it open in a jiffy."

"All right."

She trudged back to the porch, and leaned against the door frame. Good grief, what a night! Once, long ago—it seemed years ago now—she had had a lovely vision: strolls in the country, picnics by a babbling stream, her father and Mrs. Walker gazing into each other's eyes, while she and Victoria and Robert played tag and laughed in a meadow full of flowers and sunlight . . . How had that dream turned into this nightmare of frustration and panic and scurryings around in the dark? She sighed. 'If I just survive tonight,' she thought, 'nothing will ever faze me again.'

The bolt slid back with a stealthy scrape, the door opened, and she was inside.

"All set!" Robert whispered. "I unlocked the back door, too. Here's the closet key, so I can let Vicky out. It doesn't *exactly* fit, but if you kind of lift it at the same time you turn it, it usually works. I'll go up and tell her what the plan is."

"Good! I'll call up the elev—"

"Great Caesar!" Robert hissed, clutching her arm. "Somebody's moving around up there!"

They crouched and listened. There were quiet shuffling footsteps somewhere on the second floor, and a wavering glow of candlelight was approaching the top of the stairs.

"Into the parlor!" Robert whispered.

They ducked behind the sofa and watched. It was Maggie, padding downstairs in carpet slippers, a robe several sizes too big for her, and a frilled cap tied under the chin. She was carrying a candlestick in one hand, and a large gleaming china pitcher in the other. She yawned as she passed by the parlor entrance.

"Going to fill her pitcher," Robert whispered. "I'll charge upstairs while she's in the kitchen. Get the elevator ready as soon as the coast is clear. We'll be down as soon as we can."

"Right! I'll be waiting for you."

He tiptoed to the parlor entrance, glanced down the hallway, and then silently vanished up the stairs.

"Klunk-ump, klunk-ump," the pump in the kitchen complained.

Susan took a step toward the other hallway, the one where the elevator was, and hesitated. Could she risk it yet? Maggie might come back that way . . .

Oh—good—*grief!* Her hands were empty—at some

point during all the hurly-burly outside she had lost her pillowcase and her *Harper's Bazar. Now* what was she going to use to wedge the elevator door open? She was going to have to find something, quick! Her trembling hands felt along the surfaces of plush, brocade, polished wood . . . This box wouldn't work, this vase wouldn't, wasn't there *any*thing—?

Oh, oh, Maggie was coming back—candlelight was

wavering down the hallway by the stairs. Susan dove behind the sofa, and peeked over the back. Maggie shuffled into view, leaning a little to the right under the weight of her pitcher.

Crash! A door was hurled open upstairs.

Both Susan and Maggie jumped. Maggie's candle

dipped so wildly that it almost went out, and a dollop of water from her pitcher splashed on the floor.

"Robert!" Cousin Jane's voice snapped. "What are you doing out of your room? How did you open that door? Answer me, sir!"

Another door banged open.

"Isabelle! Will you kindly look at this? Do you see what comes of relaxing discipline even for an instant? Oh! *Oh!* Victoria! What are *you* doing with your door open? Isabelle, this is an outrage! These children are *defying* me! I will not have it! Robert! *Robert!*"

Robert came bolting down the stairs like a rabbit. His momentum carried him into the front door with a glass-rattling smash. He rebounded, dodged around Maggie— another dip of the candle, another splash of water on the floor—and disappeared down the hallway.

"Mer-r-ciful hivvens!" Maggie exclaimed.

"Come back here this instant, you ruffian!" Cousin Jane shouted. "Return at once or I shall come down and fetch you! If you put me to that trouble, I promise you that you will never forget it!"

"Jane!" Mrs. Walker's voice cried. "I have reached the end of my tether! Don't you dare touch that boy!"

"I see my duty and I intend to do it!"

"Jane—!"

"Interfere with me at your peril."

Down the stairs Cousin Jane stormed, in a red flannel robe and a nightcap. She carried a candle in one hand and brandished her umbrella in the other. Even in the soft candlelight her eyes and pince-nez glasses seemed to glitter. Mrs. Walker and Victoria came running down behind her.

"What are you doing here, you nincompoop?" Cousin Jane shouted at Maggie. "Why didn't you stop him?"

"Sure, Mum, with both me hands full? And himself passin' by like a cannonball?"

"Imbeciles!" Cousin Jane raged. "I am surrounded by imbeciles! Where did he go?"

"Sure, Mum, how could I tell with him skinnin' out so fast he was gone before I could turn me head?"

"If you touch that child, Jane," Mrs. Walker said quietly, "I shall—I don't know what!"

"Sure," Maggie said, lifting her chin, "and whatever it is, Mum, I'll help ye!"

"Your wages will be stopped as of this instant," Cousin Jane snapped. "As for *you*, Isabelle, I shall deal with you later." Suddenly, with amazing agility for one of her stoutness, she pounced into the parlor, raising her candle as she did so. Susan was completely taken by surprise, with her face lifted above the back of the sofa. She shrank with a squeak of dismay.

"Aha!" Cousin Jane cried. "You thought to outwit *me*, did you? Stand up, you heathen! You insubordinate— Oh! It's that Shaw baggage! *What are you doing here?*"

Her umbrella was poised to strike. Her glasses glittered like the eyes of a serpent. Susan began to back away on legs that threatened to buckle under her. "I—" she croaked.

"This is a plot," Cousin Jane hissed. "I can smell it. And Robert is implicated too, isn't he? You have corrupted him, haven't you? Oh, I saw right through you and your father the minute I laid eyes on you. A precious pair of scoundrels and thieves! Where is he? What are you up to? What are you doing in this house? Where is Robert?"

Susan, backing away, stumbled over a hassock, staggered a few steps, grabbed out with both hands to keep from falling, and seized something that bore her weight.

174

Fringed portieres . . . She was in the doorway of the hall. She continued to retreat before Cousin Jane's implacable advance. The grandfather clock ticked and tocked as though nothing were passing but time.

"*Out* with it! *Out* with it!" Cousin Jane cried, slashing with her umbrella. The steel tip whistled in a downward arc one inch from Susan's face.

The door at the other end of the hallway opened.

"What's that? Who's that?" Cousin Jane snapped. She stopped, lifted her candle, and peered past Susan into the shadows. Maggie came up by Cousin Jane's left side; she was moaning, and her round eyes were fixed on Susan. Mrs. Walker stopped one pace behind. Victoria, waxen-faced, stared over their shoulders.

"Aha!" Cousin Jane said. "Exactly! That scoundrel Shaw! And another villain! Oh, yes, quite a little plot, isn't it?"

Susan turned. Her father, looking very strange, was coming into the light, followed by Mr. Sweeney. He was soaking wet. His hair was plastered down over his skull, his boots made squelching noises, his lovely suit was dark and clinging and festooned with water-weed. And oh!—oh!

Did Mr. Sweeney have in his hand what she thought he had?

Yes . . .

Susan's legs would not hold her up any longer, and she collapsed against the wainscotting.

⋙ 21. MR. SHAW GOES UNDER ⋘

*. . . told us that his part of the plan went
pretty well at first. Mr. Sweeney was
suspicious, but Daddy calmed him down
until the police came with that runaway
boy. Mr. Sweeney insisted on going to the
house to find out what was happening. Mr.
Hollister fired as they began to cross the
yard, and from then on everything got out
of hand for Daddy too . . .*

"Sweeney? Sweeney?"

There was no answer. The stable was empty.

"Good night!" Mr. Shaw muttered. He groped through
the dimness until he came to a manger, where he sat
down.

Was Sweeney going to show up, or had the plan mis-
carried? Mr. Shaw rather hoped the latter. Throughout
the afternoon his original enthusiasm had been slowly
giving away before the onslaught of doubts and scruples.
He was a law-abiding man, after all, with small taste
for either violence or deceit. Sweeney would come to no
physical harm in the elevator; but still, to be snatched
from your own century and hurled into another was a
serious matter.

So was taking the law into one's own hands . . .

But then the vision that had been haunting him ever
since last night suddenly glowed in his imagination
again: Isabelle Walker, her tumbled hair glinting in
candlelight, her cheeks wet with tears . . . His heart
leaped. And yet the man he was worrying about could

pretend to pay court to her for the purpose of stealing every last thing she had! And without a qualm! Mr. Shaw could hear that smooth voice saying, "Why, she has her house and plenty of leisure. Let her take in boarders, or do laundry, or something . . ."

Ah, the dog! Feel scruples about *him*? His fists clenched. At that instant a quiet footfall sounded, and a low voice said, "Shaw?"

Mr. Shaw, trembling with rage, had all he could do to keep from hurling himself on Mr. Sweeney. "Here," he grated.

Mr. Sweeney crunched over the straw until the pale oval of his face was visible. He leaned against a post. His voice was intense and quiet. He said, "Look here, Shaw, I want an explanation!"

"About what?"

"That business this afternoon with the policeman."

"Oh. It's nothing to do with us. Robert disappeared for a while, that's all."

"Why? He was supposed to be playing with the girls."

"They, ah, had a quarrel, and that cousin who's staying with them lectured him about manners. So he went off to sulk, and the ladies thought he'd run away, and called in the police. And then he came home again, and it all blew over."

"I didn't see the boy going anywhere," Mr. Sweeney said. "Or coming back either."

"Well, you can't watch everywhere at once, can you?"

"But I did see you consulting with the police!"

"Sweeney, don't be a flaming fool. I know you've been watching me. If I wanted to bring the police into our business, I wouldn't do it right in front of you. I spoke to that policeman simply to find out what he was doing here. In fact, I suspected *you* were behind it. I thought maybe you'd changed your mind and denounced us after all."

There was a short silence. Then Mr. Sweeney said, "That won't do. If you really thought you'd been denounced, you wouldn't have walked out into the arms of the police like that. You'd have made your escape."

"Sweeney," Mr. Shaw sighed, "your suspicions bore me. I've given you my explanation; you can take it or leave it. If you think something funny is going on, why aren't you making *your* escape?"

"Ah!" Mr. Sweeney said. "Ah! You were just hoping I'd do that, weren't you, Shaw? That's your game, isn't it? And then you'd have the jewels all to yourself, wouldn't you? Well, abandon that hope, Shaw. I'm staying right here. We will proceed as planned."

"You know, Sweeney, one might be led to conclude that you don't trust me."

"Oh, perish the thought, Shaw! I trust you implicitly —mainly because I know that *you* know how hot I can make it for you if you try to betray me. That means in *any particular,* Shaw. Do we understand each other?"

"I guess we do."

"Excellent!" There was a rustling noise as if Mr. Sweeney were taking something out of his pocket, and then the faint tinkling of a little bell.

"What's that?"

"My repeater," Mr. Sweeney said impatiently. "What's the matter with you, Shaw? Nerves?"

"No, it just, ah, took me by surprise." 'Repeater . . . ?' he wondered.

"Mmm. After nine. We have some waiting to do, Shaw. We might as well do it comfortably." And Mr. Sweeney threw himself down on the straw.

Repeater! Of course—it was a watch that struck the

time when you pressed a button . . . Mr. Shaw sighed, and sat down on the straw himself. Yes, they *would* proceed as planned. He felt no more doubts, no more scruples. The very tone of Mr. Sweeney's voice had cured him of those.

They waited.

⊰⊰ ⊰⊰ ⊰⊰ ⊱⊱ ⊱⊱ ⊱⊱

"Hullo!" Mr. Sweeney said when they heard the horse and buggy stop out in front of the house.

They held their breath and listened. There was a long silence; then the faint snap of a whip and the sound of the horse cantering away.

"Something peculiar here, Shaw," Mr. Sweeney muttered.

"There certainly is. They wouldn't be having visitors at this time of night, would they? What time is it, anyway?"

Mr. Sweeney's repeater tinkled. "Almost twelve!" he exclaimed. "Look here, Shaw, you didn't arrange to have someone drop in on us, did you?"

"Oh, don't be an idiot!"

Mr. Sweeney breathed hard for a few minutes, then said, "I want to know what's going on."

"So do I. What do you suggest we do?"

"I believe we'd better go to the house and investigate. This could seriously affect our plans, Shaw."

"I know."

They stood up. Mr. Shaw bit his lip. What *was* happening at the house, anyway? His heart hammered against his ribs as he reflected that any kind of disturbance could upset the plan completely. They stepped out of the stable. Good lord, how bright the moon was!

Mr. Sweeney nodded toward some ghostly white bushes, and they headed for the nearest one.

"Stop, thieves!"

They froze.

"Oh, good night!" Mr. Shaw muttered. "It's that flaming fool, Hollister!"

"Horse thieves! Cutthroats!" Mr. Hollister bawled from the second floor of his house. *"Don't move—I've got you in my sights, you Republican sneaks!"*

Mr. Sweeney soundlessly melted behind a bush. "Down!" he whispered.

"Oh, you will, will you?" Mr. Hollister brayed.

Mr. Shaw, still immobile in his tracks, staring at Hollisters' house, saw a bright orange flash erupt in an upstairs window. There was a terrific blast. Mr. Shaw felt an urgent desire to be on the other side of something solid. He jumped for the nearest bush. Too small, too thin! A hedge loomed nearby. He hurled himself into it, through it. Something glimmered in front of him. His foot caught on a low stone parapet, and he fell, clawing the air for support. Then he struck—but not moonlit turf as he had expected. Down he went, with an involuntary gasp that half filled his lungs with water. He was drowning! He touched mud, gave a mighty kick, shot up into the air, and found himself standing waist-deep in a pond. He gagged and spat out a stream of stagnant-tasting water.

Mr. Sweeney hissed "Imbecile!" and seized his hands and hauled him out. They crouched behind the hedge that bordered the pond, and listened. Silence had returned to the world.

It was broken by a door banging open at Hollisters'. In a moment they heard a faint braying in front of the Walker house; then another interval of silence; then

Hollisters' door again.

"Hail, the conquering hero," Mr. Sweeney sneered. "I expect they're all going to be up now, appreciating his heroism. Awkward . . . I know your daughter will be keeping cool during the uproar, however."

"Oh, I'm sure she, ah—"

"She's such an artist, she could even turn it into an advantage. No opportunity like a moment or two of confusion for dipping into the jewel box, eh? Well, let's give them a little time to settle down, and then carry on with our investigating."

"Ah, all right."

"I detect a certain lack of conviction in your tone, Shaw. One might even say, an outright reluctance."

"Oh—oh, no. It's just that I, ah—all this noise and so forth has—shaken me up a bit."

"Perhaps your little aquatic excursion has had, shall we say, a *dampening* effect? Well, these things will happen. One must exercise one's philosophy, Shaw."

'Oh, go this, that, and the other, you weasel!' Mr. Shaw raged to himself. 'What the *devil* am I going to do now?'

The plan just couldn't work now that everyone in the house was aroused and on edge. Oh, *blast* that idiot Hollister! Of course he had told them what he had seen in their back yard; and even if they went back to bed immediately, their nerves would be stretched tight. The slightest sound in the house would have them all up and about instantly . . . Maybe he should call off the whole thing until tomorrow night.

"Come along, Shaw," Mr. Sweeney murmured, standing up. "Once more into the breach."

"Look," Mr. Shaw began, "how about—?"

There was a crash in the shrubbery beside the house.

Cats began to yowl and thrash about in combat. A window was thrown open. Maggie's voice could be heard shouting in reproof. Water spattered down on leaves. The cats disengaged.

Mr. Sweeney sat down again. "More alarums and excursions. You know, Shaw, it all begins to take on a faintly comic aspect, don't you think?"

"I don't see the humor of it," Mr. Shaw muttered. Blast the man, anyway! He actually seemed to be enjoying all this! "Look," he began again. "It occurs to me that Susan may not have gotten the chance to, ah, do it, what with all these interruptions. Don't you think we—?"

"Oh, I have complete faith in that daughter of yours, Shaw."

"Well, ah, I do too, of course. It's just that everybody will be so nervous and jumpy in there that— And if we don't show up, she'll know just what to do. Then tomorrow night we can—"

Mr. Sweeney laughed quietly. "Shaw," he said, "the trouble with you is that you are so childishly transparent. I've been in this profession a long time, my dear fellow, and no one can catch me twice with the same tricks."

"What?"

"I will admit that these disturbances have been very competently staged. Of course, while you were in town today you might have made arrangements for a brass band and a fire brigade, too—or did you? Perhaps they're in the wings now, waiting for their cue. And I must say that your own acting is first-rate—all this pretense of reluctance and nervousness."

Mr. Shaw was having difficulty catching up. "Now wait a minute," he said. "Staged? Do you actually think that I—?"

"Come off it, Shaw," Mr. Sweeney sighed. "You and Susan frightened me away once with a rigged-up scene. Now that I know how you operate, it's not going to work a second time. I am *not* coming back tomorrow night only to find that you two have flown the coop—with the jewels, of course. And since you are so reluctant to share, I might as well confess that *I* don't enjoy sharing, either. I want those jewels myself, Shaw. All of them."

Mr. Sweeney took his hand out of his pocket. There was a chilling *click*. Mr. Shaw found himself looking into the muzzle of a revolver.

"Forward march, Shaw! No use tempting Hollister into any more acts of heroism, so we'll just take a roundabout route until the house covers us, and then double back. Now please don't oblige me to shoot you, my dear fellow—it's so unprofessional and unphilosophical."

⊰{ 22. THE BATTLE OF ELEVATOR HALL }⊱

> *. . . turned into a terrific struggle after Bobbie tipped the scales. I guess all that water saved us, really, because it made everybody skid and fall so much. Otherwise Mr. Sweeney might have gotten away and Cousin Jane wouldn't have "sealed her own fate," as Vicky puts it . . .*

"Mer-r-cy on us!" Maggie quavered. Her candle performed wild figures in the air. "It's them Shaws! And that Mr. Sweeney!"

"Steady, Maggie," Mrs. Walker said in a quiet voice. "There's nothing to be afraid of."

"Sure and I'm stiddy as I can be, Mum, with me second sight tellin' me them Shaws are a sign."

Mr. Shaw looked at Susan and lifted his shoulders in a gesture of despair. "I'm sorry, chick," he muttered. "Everything went to pieces out there. Mrs. Walker, I hope I'll have an opportunity to explain, or *try* to expl—"

"Your explanations are not wanted," Cousin Jane snapped. "You are a scoundrel, and that is all *we* need to know. I thought I had made my prohibition clear. And yet I find your daughter creeping about in the dark like a thief, and subverting the Walker children; and I find *you* up to who knows what villainies, prating meanwhile of 'explanations.' There can be no explanations under these circumstances. You are to leave this house instantly. *And* your daughter. And you too, whoever *you* are!"

Mr. Sweeney raised his derby and said, "I have not had the pleasure of making your acquaintance, Madame."

"And I have no wish to make *yours*, sir! You are an impertinent scalawag! Leave this house at once, all of you! And be assured that I intend to notify the police about your actions immediately."

"I am trembling in my boots, Madame," Mr. Sweeney said in his smoothest voice. His lips twitched as though he were suppressing a smile. He turned his eyes to the others. "Well! Quite an *omnium gatherum!* How are you, Maggie? Please accept my apologies for any lost sleep this may cause you. Isabelle! I didn't think I'd have the pleasure of seeing you again. Such a pity that we have to meet under these awkward circumstances! Ah—that fiery light in your eyes—enchanting!"

"I know what to think of you, sir," Mrs. Walker said.

"Quite so. Victoria, my dear! You look frightened. There is no need to be apprehensive, you know. As long as you all behave, no harm will come to any of you. Now, who is missing? Oh, yes, Robert! Still sleeping after the rigors of the day, I presume. Such an active little fellow!"

"My patience is at an end!" Cousin Jane shouted. "I have undergone shouting and shots in the night and impertinences and disobedience and base ingratitude and loss of sleep. This effrontery is the last intolerable straw! Get out!" She took a step forward and raised her umbrella.

"Madame," Mr. Sweeney said with venomous intensity, "my patience is no more elastic than yours. Do you see what I have in my hand? If you don't step back and hold your tongue, I will shoot this gentleman. And if *his* life is of no consequence to you, *yours* will instantly follow."

"Jane!" Mrs. Walker said. "I'm afraid that Mr. Sweeney means exactly what he says. Please do what he asks."

"Very well, Isabelle—for your sake, not for mine. *I* have nothing but scorn for his threats." Cousin Jane stepped back beside Maggie and lowered her umbrella. Her face was dark with rage. "*Scoundrel!*" she hissed.

"That I am, Madame," Mr. Sweeney said, flashing his most brilliant smile. "It is my calling in life, and I glory in it. But I take no pleasure in forcing my company on those who don't welcome it, so I shall detain you no longer than absolutely necessary. Susan, my dear, where is it?"

"What?" she croaked.

"Oh, come, girl—you know what I mean. The cloth bag!"

Good grief, what was she going to do now? "Cuk—cuk—cloth bag?" she stammered, shrinking back against the wainscotting. Something in the wall gave way under the pressure of her shoulder blade.

"Sweeney, let her alone," Mr. Shaw said. "There isn't any cloth bag. There aren't any jewels. The whole thing was a—"

"Still trying to put me off, Shaw? Your persistence is admirable, but I'm beginning to find it tiresome."

"Sweeney, you flaming ass, don't you understand? There *isn't*—"

"Shut up, Shaw. Susan, bring me that bag. If the jewels aren't in a bag yet, bring me the box—and your key, too. You have two minutes. If you are not back by then, your father is a dead man."

'I can fix up another pillowcase!' she thought. 'I can throw some of Vicky's things in. At least it'll give us some time to—' "I'll—I'll get it," she said, staggering forward a step.

Behind her the wainscotting split open with the old familiar rumble and sigh. A harsh glare of electric light flooded the hallway.

Everyone gasped.

"Oh, good night!" Mr. Shaw muttered at the ceiling. "That's all we need!"

"Mer-r-rciful hivvens!" Maggie moaned. Her eyes turned up in their sockets, the candle and pitcher fell from her hands, and her body toppled over backward. Mrs. Walker caught her by the shoulders just in time, and, staggering under her weight, eased her to the floor.

Maggie's pitcher landed on Cousin Jane's left foot with a crunchy thud, and fell over, sending a gush of water across the parquet floor. Cousin Jane shrieked and doubled over. Her candle fell to the floor, and her pince-nez glasses, popping off her nose, bounced at the end of their black ribbon. She shrieked again, a long soaring crescendo that made the glass front of the grandfather clock rattle, and hopped backwards, putting out her free hand for support. Mrs. Walker's shoulder was the first thing that came within reach. She seized it and leaned. Mrs. Walker, still in the act of kneeling by Maggie, dropped suddenly to her knees under Cousin Jane's weight, and for an instant it looked as if both of them would collapse in a heap.

Victoria scurried forward and lifted Cousin Jane upright again.

"Ooooooh! My foot! Send for the doctor! Get me to a chair!"

"There're chairs in the parlor, Cousin Jane," Victoria quavered. "If I hold you up, do you think you can hop—?"

"No!" Mr. Sweeney said. "No one will leave this hallway but Susan. The rest of you will stay exactly where you are."

"You are a heartless villain, sir!" Victoria flashed out. "She is in pain!"

"She may endure it standing as well as sitting. You are not to move."

He turned to Mrs. Walker with that familiar smile of ironic appreciation. "Well, Isabelle! What a consummate deceiver you are! I knew you were wealthy, but I would never in a thousand years have suspected that you possessed electric lighting. And a closet with self-opening doors! That's affluence on a grand scale! Well, my dear, this excessive wealth must be a burden to you, so I am going to relieve you of some of it. Susan, why are you dawdling? Fetch me that jewelry, girl. One minute left, and your father's life hangs in the balance!"

"I—I'm going," Susan gulped. She was rooted to the spot. She was trying not to look directly at what was happening, trying not to betray to Mr. Sweeney the fact that—that—

"Push, somebody," Robert said.

He had crept down the hallway from the kitchen, quiet as a moth, and had gone down on his hands and knees just behind, and broadside to, Mr. Sweeney's legs.

Mr. Sweeney turned his head with a little snort of

surprise. For an instant the muzzle of his revolver was not pointed at Mr. Shaw's ribs. Susan, feeling as though she were in a dream, as though she were moving under water, as though she were someone else watching a stranger named Susan doing something that was more dangerous than anything she had ever done in her life —Susan stepped forward one long step, and laid both her hands against Mr. Sweeney's chest, and shoved.

Mr. Sweeney toppled backwards over Robert in an almost leisurely arc, his mouth opening and his eyes widening as he went. There was a loud explosion from his pistol. Two of the paper flowers in the vase (on the marble-topped table with the carved lyre-shaped legs) leaped up and turned into fragments, and a windowpane in the parlor shivered out of its frame with a sweet silvery tinkle.

Mrs. Walker and Victoria screamed.

Mr. Sweeney hit the floor with a crash and a grunt, and his derby flew off. Mr. Shaw pounced on him, and snarled in a high choking voice, "Call her *Isabelle*, will you, you slimy rat!" He grabbed Mr. Sweeney's right wrist in one hand, and pommeled his face with the other. Mr. Sweeney said "Aagh!" and seized Mr. Shaw's cravat. They grappled and rolled together.

"This is an outrage!" Cousin Jane shouted. She pounded the floor with the tip of her umbrella. "Why has no one fetched me a chair? Why has no one gone for the doctor? Isabelle, turn those ruffians out of the house at once, and attend to my needs!"

But Mrs. Walker paid no attention. Her lower lip was crushed between her teeth, and her eyes were fixed on Robert. He was lying face down on the floor, trying to protect his head with his arms as the battle-locked forms of the two men rolled and grunted on top of him.

"Mmf fm mumpf!" came his voice from the melee.

"What?" Susan cried. She hovered on the edge of the fight, looking for her chance to jump in and help her father, but aware that if she jumped at the wrong instant she would only hinder him.

"*Umm!*" Robert said.

"Gun!" Mr. Shaw gasped by way of translation. "Get—" and then his voice was cut off as they rolled over again. But here was Susan's chance. Her father was forcing Mr. Sweeney's hand, the one that held the pistol, down toward the floor. She stamped on it with her heel. Mr. Sweeney shouted, and the pistol came loose. Then Robert's knee appeared out of the scrimmage and struck the pistol, and sent it spinning across the floor toward the red velvet window curtains. It created a confused wake as it plowed through the puddle of water from Maggie's pitcher. Susan leaped for it—tried to leap for it. The wet floor was as slippery as ice. Her feet shot out from under her, and she landed on her back with a jolt that knocked most of the breath out of her lungs.

A kind of buzzing roar filled her ears for a moment as she gasped air back into her chest again. She raised her head, and looked around in time to see Mr. Sweeney staggering to his feet. Her father, balanced shakily on one knee, was drawing back his arm for another blow. His fist flashed through the air. Mr. Sweeney, either intentionally or because his feet were skidding in the water, dodged the blow. The momentum of Mr. Shaw's swinging arm carried him around in a semicircle; he lost his balance and went down on his chest with a grunt. Mr. Sweeney lurched forward, stumbled over Susan, got to his feet again instantly, and took two great slippery steps that brought him close to Victoria and Cousin

Jane.

"Stop or I'll shoot!" Robert squeaked.

Mr. Sweeney glanced back, and froze.

Robert was on his knees by the window curtains. He held the revolver in both shaking hands; and even as Mr. Sweeney turned his head, one of Robert's thumbs pulled back the hammer.

All was silent. Slowly, slowly, Mr. Sweeney turned around.

"Well!" he said quietly, with a slight smile on his lips. "What do you wish me to do, Robert? Perhaps Mr. Shaw could make a suggestion."

Without thinking, Robert turned to Mr. Shaw. Mr. Sweeney hurled himself on Victoria—but his foot slipped in the water as he pounced; and instead of seizing her firmly as he had intended, he fell toward her, saving himself from going down only by clutching her shoulder with both hands. She screamed and twisted away from his grasp; her feet skidded backwards; she fell to her knees. Deprived of their support, Cousin Jane and Mr. Sweeney toppled toward each other, and embraced. They swayed for a moment, dancing around Victoria, frantically trying to maintain balance. Their gyrations carried them forward a few steps. Cousin Jane cried out as her injured foot momentarily took her weight. Then Mr. Sweeney regained control. He spun Cousin Jane in a half-circle so that he was behind her; hugged her tightly, pinning her arms to her sides; then heaved her about to position her stout body between himself and Robert.

Robert lowered the pistol.

"Let me—*go*, you cur!" Cousin Jane gasped. She still had a grip on her umbrella; but without the use of her arms, she could only tap Mr. Sweeney on the leg with it by waggling her wrist.

"With pleasure—Madame," Mr. Sweeney panted. "But only—when we—reach—the parlor. Backward—march!"

He tried to pull her backwards. It might have worked with Victoria, but Cousin Jane was too heavy. "Wretch!" she cried. "Let *go!*" and she flung her whole weight forward.

The locked forms swayed, and went down in a slow arc, Mr. Sweeney on the bottom, Cousin Jane on top, through the elevator door. The impact of their bodies on the floor made the elevator jangle and bounce in its shaft.

The wainscotting sighed, and began to rumble shut. "Hey!" Mr. Shaw shouted. "Stop it! *Get* it!"

He and Susan lunged for the elevator on hands and knees. Susan was closer, but even so she was almost too late. The door nipped her hand in its rubber-edged bite; then the safety device wheezed, and the door recoiled.

"Hold it open!" Mr. Shaw panted. He struggled to his feet and skidded toward the elevator.

Cousin Jane rolled away from Mr. Sweeney's prostrate form, sat up, and replaced her pince-nez. "Out*rage*ous!" she hissed through clenched teeth. "I'll make them pay for this!"

Susan threw herself against the folded-back door. It bunted against her palms, protesting: *wheeze-grumf, wheeze-grumf.*

"Miss Clamp!" Mr. Shaw cried. "Get out of there!"

"Scoundrel!" she shouted. "Leave this house at once! And take your gutter-brat with you!"

"You don't understand! You have to get *out!*" And Mr. Shaw reached forward to pull her clear.

"Don't touch me!" she spat. Her umbrella whistled

through the air and struck him squarely in the face. With a cry he staggered back, and fell.

"*Daddy!*" Susan screamed. She scrabbled over the floor toward him.

The door began to trundle shut again.

Mr. Sweeney struggled to his feet, gasping for air, and lurched toward the narrowing exit.

Cousin Jane roared, "Don't you *dare* close this door!" and began to pound a deafening tattoo on it with her umbrella.

"Back!" Robert cried, leveling the revolver.

Mr. Sweeney, supporting his weight with his right hand, which had unknowingly come to rest on the control buttons, paused groggily for an instant—a fatal instant.

The wainscotting closed, plunging the hallway into darkness, and the resonant *bang bang bang* of Cousin Jane's umbrella faded away into silence.

❄❄❄ ❄❄❄ ❄❄❄ ❄❄❄ ❄❄❄ ❄❄❄

For a long time nothing could be heard but the ticking of the grandfather clock and the sounds of heavy breathing. The smell of gunsmoke still hung in the air.

"Are you all right, Daddy?" Susan quavered.

"Think so . . . Whew, what a clout! Is she gone?"

"Yes."

"Oh, lord . . ."

In a low, shaking voice Mrs. Walker said, "Have we all gone mad, Mr. Shaw?"

"Oh no, oh no! It's all explainable, sort of." They could hear him struggling into a sitting position. "Mrs. Walker . . . I guess this is going to sound irrelevant. Please forgive me. Did your cousin have a middle name?"

"Yes: Hildegarde."

"Ah! Hmm . . ."

"Where has she gone, Mr. Shaw?"

"Well, ah, it's hard to explain, Mrs. Walker. She's gone very far away. I don't believe any harm will come to her, but she won't come back. Ever. I'm sorry."

"Oh." Mrs. Walker was silent for a while, and then said in a very low voice, "Perhaps it is wicked of me, but—but if it is true that she will come to no harm, then I cannot bring myself to feel sorry that she won't return."

"Nor can I," Victoria said shakily.

"Me neither!" Robert declared.

Click whirrr, said the clock, and its sweet melancholy chime announced that the new day was three-quarters of an hour old.

"Vicky, dear, you're closest to the parlor. Will you please bring in a candle?"

"Yes, Mama."

For a long time they listened to Victoria bumping around in the dark, and the *skritch skritch* of her shaking hands striking one match after another in the attempt to light a candle. At last she succeeded, and a soft orange glow came wavering back into the hallway, and they could all see each other again.

Mrs. Walker still knelt by Maggie, and was chafing her wrists. Mr. Shaw sat leaning back on his arms, with a smile dawning on his face—the smile of a man who realizes that all obstacles have been removed from his path.

"By George!" he murmured. "By *George!*" He got to his feet, shuffling to keep his balance in the water slick. "Corporal," he said, catching sight of Robert, "we'd better lay down our arms, don't you think?" He took the revolver from Robert, uncocked it carefully, and laid it on

194

the marble-topped table. "That gun might have been the end of me. Corporal—no, I think from now on we should say 'Sergeant.' Sergeant, you saved my life, I think. Thank you."

Robert blinked solemnly and reddened as they shook hands.

"Vicky, Susie, you were both enormously courageous. Good work, and thank you!"

Susan and Victoria slopped and slid toward each other, and fell into each other's arms, and began to laugh and cry at the same time.

"Great Caesar!" Robert muttered, trying to look disgusted, but swallowing hard.

"As for me—well, you may all take turns kicking me. How *could* I have concocted such an asinine plan?"

"Oh, it was a capital plan, sir! It's just that the unexpected always happens during a battle."

"Well, thank goodness you kids knew how to take advantage of the unexpected! Mrs. Walker, I owe you an explanation."

"An explanation would be most welcome, Mr. Shaw."

"Oh my, oh my! It's such a long story!" Despite his soaking clothes and plastered-down hair and a raw contusion on his forehead, Susan had never seen him looking so handsome and happy. He glowed with excitement, like another candle. "I don't think you're going to believe it. I don't think *I'm* going to believe it. You see, we—but before I tell you all that, I want to tell you something else. And *then* I'll tell you why we—what we—oh, good night, where do I begin?"

"Begin with the elevator, sir!" Robert cried. "It goes through time, Mama! It travels to the *future!*"

"It really begins with Mr. Sweeney!" Victoria said. "It was Susan who unmasked him, Mama! We suspected he was a scoundrel, but she's the one who really proved it!"

"It really begins with the witch," Susan put in. "At least our part of it. You see, Mrs. Walker, we couldn't even have come here if she hadn't given me three trips—"

"But I had to go to the wishing well before she did that. And I had to go *again*, yesterday—no, day before yesterday—"

"And we had a treasure map, Mama, and it was from a newspaper in *1960!*"

"And we found the treasure!"

"Only we lost it again."

"But I know where his camp is, and I'll bet it's there! That's why I was away so long, Mama, but I couldn't tell you in front of Cousin Jane."

"Goodness!" Mrs. Walker said, looking from one face to another. "The more you tell me, the less I understand. You seem to have been up to a great deal behind my back!"

"Oh, yes!" Mr. Shaw laughed. "It's a regular conspiracy. Our children are deep-dyed plotters, Mrs. Walker. I didn't know anything about it myself until they had it all settled among themselves what our fate was to be."

"*Our* fate, Mr. Shaw?"

Victoria and Susan glanced at each other and began to giggle.

"Yes, our fate. Believe me, I resisted as long as I could. You may resist too, but it'll be useless. You can't win against these three!"

"I am more confused than ever, Mr. Shaw."

"Oh, I can understand it. I'm trying to un-confuse you as fast as I can. That's why I started to say what I started to say a few minutes ago. I'll say it again. I'm going to warn you, now, that I am *going* to say, later— I mean, so it won't be so much of a shock then—later, that is— What I *mean* is, after all the explanations are explained, and everything, I'm going to ask you to marry me."

Susan sucked in her breath and looked at Mrs. Walker.

But Mrs. Walker did not recoil, or faint, or scream. She said, "Oh." Perhaps she flushed a little—it was hard to tell in candlelight. She kept her gaze steadily on Mr. Shaw. She said, "I think I'd better put on some water for tea. Vicky, will you take care of Maggie, please? Bobbie, we'll need the smelling salts again—they're in my room." She stood up.

Mr. Shaw offered his arm and said, "The floor is awfully slippery."

She looked at him gravely for a moment. "Well, my children trust you implicitly, it seems. I believe I can, too." She gave him a little smile, and laid her hand on his arm, and said, "The kitchen is that way. Lead on, Mr. Shaw."

◄§ 23. AN OLD PHOTOGRAPH REVIEWED ∦►

Susan's diary doesn't end with her father helping Mrs. Walker along the slippery floor of the hallway. There is more. I'll get back to it as soon as I've mentioned some other matters.

For instance, there is the question of what became of Mr. Sweeney. All I can do about that is to report my speculations and, in a moment, a wild surmise.

I assume that when the elevator stopped again after Mr. Bodoni sent it up from the basement, Mr. Sweeney escaped. He would have had to come within range of Cousin Jane's umbrella to do so, and I'll wager that she gave him a couple of good thwacks as he scrambled out. Perhaps he brushed against the basement button in passing, and thus sent the elevator on its final descent. Very likely he lurked about in the building for a while, wondering where he was. Eventually he must have wandered out into the street, to encounter all the surprises that the twentieth century had in store for him. I hope his philosophy was equal to the occasion . . . But then, the Sweeneys of this world usually land on their feet; and I conjecture that it didn't take him long to discover that he could make use of his professional talents as well in this century as in the last.

Cousin Jane, I regret to say, came into the twentieth century a wealthy woman.

Although Mr. Shaw and Mrs. Walker were not sorry that she was gone, it did bother their consciences that she would be plunged into the twentieth century without any means of support. So after some careful thought, Mr. Shaw set up a small trust fund in a bank that he knew would be reliable—the Tri-City Guaranty and Trust Company—and deposited sealed instructions in their vaults. The envelope was to be opened on a certain Tuesday of March, 1960—that is, three days after the Shaws had disappeared in the elevator. Mr. Shaw could not know, of course, that matters at this end would be delayed a year and a half. (More about that delay in a moment.) But the Special Notice did make him realize that for some reason Cousin Jane might be difficult to locate. So the instructions were that on the following day, the bank should look for Jane Hildegarde Clamp (carefully described as to physical appearance, dress, and state of mind) in the Ward Street apartment building; and that if she were not found, the bank should advertise for her whereabouts. That was why the Special Notice had been running in the papers for so long.

It fell to me to give the Tri-City Guaranty and Trust Company the information it had been seeking, and to claim my reward. Cousin Jane was rescued from the Ward Street police station, and put in possession of her trust fund. It was an impressive amount of money after eighty years of growth.

I have mentioned that I don't subscribe to a newspaper, but I do look at them in the news-stands, and buy one when the occasion warrants; and as Cousin Jane's new career was of the kind that journalists delight in, I was able to follow it in some detail. It did not take her long to decide that she disapproved of the twentieth century, and that her duty toward it was clear. With her fortune she established a foundation, the Mission for the Elevation of Contemporary Moral Tone. The Mission sent workers to remote tropical islands to bully the inhabitants into wearing more clothes and improving their table manners. It showered the Laboring Classes with moral instruction in the form of tracts and pamphlets— all of which ended up as litter in the streets. It strove mightily to suppress Infamous Literature, making a serious nuisance of itself among publishers and libraries and booksellers . . .

But Cousin Jane finally met her nemesis in the form of a gentleman whose dedication to moral tone seemed as relentless as her own. He became the Mission's treasurer. Two months later he vanished with a large part of the Mission's money. He was arrested at the Mexican border, and brought to trial, and given a stiff sentence; but the money was never recovered. Cousin Jane was forced to retire into a frugal private life, leaving contemporary moral tone to shift for itself. The ex-treasurer's picture in the newspapers showed a fastidiously dressed and combed man with a beard. His name was reported to be Adelbert Swinderby; a name which suggests to me— But as I said, it is only a wild surmise on my part. I can't prove anything.

Why did the witch wait so long before bringing me into the case? I don't suppose I'll ever know for certain, but my tentative solution is that the matter simply slipped her mind for a year and a half. She *was* vague and absent-minded—Susan and I both noticed that. I think of her as one day suddenly putting her skinny fingers to her mouth and exclaiming, "Oh, dear! I was going to do something about little what's-her-name back in 1881, wasn't I? How careless of me! Well, now, let—me—see . . ." Practically speaking, it didn't matter that she was late, since the elevator could travel in time as flexibly as you or I can travel in space. Just as we can get to the Historical Association's headquarters from any point in the city, so could the elevator take my message back to the Shaws from any point of time in the twentieth century.

As for my friend Charles, he was more skeptical than ever when I posted him on all the new developments; although he did admit that my "story," as he persists in calling it, was a "good yarn." But his disbelief no longer irritates me. If it pleases him to think that he is right, then it pleases me even more to know that he is wrong; so our friendship is unimpaired.

And lastly, the elevator.

Late Sunday night I went down into the basement to pay my final respects. I patted the poor old battered conveyance, and thanked it for all it had done, and asked for one final favor. The favor was granted; or at any rate, not denied. I borrowed a screwdriver from Mr. Bodoni's workbench, and reverently took down the metal plate that says *Capacity 1500 Lbs.* It is one of my favorite keepsakes.

A crew of brisk and efficient men in green coveralls arrived Monday morning, and set to work. By the time they had finished on Wednesday afternoon, nothing was recognizable any more. The old arrows and dials had given way to lights that blinked the number of the floor. The new mechanism made very little sound—mostly a kind of discreet and well-lubricated *zzzzz*. It hurled you up or down with a speed that seemed to separate your stomach from the rest of your body. The interior of the car was grey and pastel blue, and there was a thick wall-to-wall carpet. A vent chilled you with a blast of conditioned air. Music, the kind you hear in dentists' offices and supermarkets, poured without interruption from a concealed loudspeaker.

Mr. Bodoni was delighted. "Real class, hah?" he said to everyone he met, grinning around his dead cigar. All the tenants seemed to agree.

I guess I'm a crank. I've used the stairs ever since.

Susan's diary goes on to record that early in the afternoon of the day after the Battle of Elevator Hall (as Sergeant Walker called it) everyone, including Maggie and Toby, fared forth on a treasure hunt. Maggie went because her second sight had been so triumphantly vindicated, and she was confident that her occult powers would enable her to find the gold, no matter how well it was hidden. Toby went because he was the kind of cat who becomes anxious when he sees all his people leaving the house at the same time. Sergeant Walker led the way to Mr. Sweeney's camp, and Toby brought up the rear with a series of rushes and skulks and an occasional yowl.

It turned out that Maggie's second sight was not up to this kind of work. They spent several fruitless hours poking through Mr. Sweeney's things, and under logs, and in leaf drifts and thickets. Toby turned kittenish, and dashed among them sideways with his back up, and finally capped their vexation by scooting up a tree and getting stuck. Robert had to climb after him. While he was aloft he noticed what looked like rope-ends draped over the lip of a tall hollow stump. They *were* rope-ends, although from ground level they looked like pieces of frayed bark. Everyone took hold of a rope, and hauled, and heavy bundles came up from inside the stump . . . They tried to carry Toby home in triumph, but he would have none of it. Cats don't understand that kind of ceremony.

The problem of evading Mr. Hollister's garrulity became troublesome, and eventually the Shaws went to town and followed up an advertisement in the newspaper for rooms and board. Their prospective landlady had no sooner shown them around when she collapsed on a horsehair sofa in the parlor and burst into hysterical weeping. Bit by bit they learned that she had recently been bilked of her life's savings. She could not bring herself to say how it had happened; but the name "Abernathy Swinnerton" came out between sobs and hiccups. Mr. Shaw and Susan exchanged glances over her head. They took the rooms at once, and Mr. Shaw made arrangements at his bank for full restitution.

He also hired a horse and trap from the local livery stable, and took driving lessons, and practiced on daily trips to and from the Walkers'.

Five days after the Battle of Elevator Hall, Mrs. Walker said yes to Mr. Shaw. Victoria claimed that *her* sharp romantic eye had already detected the state of her Mama's feelings as early as the first hour of the treasure hunt. In any case, there were proprieties to be observed, and the engagement period proceeded in the approved leisurely fashion of the time. There were long strolls and rides through the countryside; some by moonlight, and shopping expeditions, and picnics on the grassy banks of streams, and tea and cakes and ices in the garden at dusk: everything, in short, that Susan had dreamed about and yearned for.

So the summer passed, and autumn came; and on a bright blue-and-gold day in October, Mrs. Walker became Mrs. Shaw.

Susan's interest in her diary begins to taper off after this. The entries become shorter and farther apart in time. They mention sleigh rides and snowball fights; magic lantern shows; the purchase of a family mare, named Lady Jones at first, and later, when her true character began to come out, Lazy Bones; Mr. Shaw's provision for Cousin Jane in the twentieth century (a long entry here: the solution obviously intrigued Susan. I'm glad she never knew about the dreadful Mission); Maggie's betrothal to the policeman who had brought her back from town that afternoon when Robert was stalking Mr. Sweeney; schooldays; the restoration of the garden around the house; the birth of a little brother . . .

The last entry is dated September 30, 1882. It mentions various small matters, and tells about the visit of a photographer. She must have been interrupted while writing, because the final sentence says, "He also took some pictures of" Of . . . ? The house, maybe, or Lazy Bones, or Toby—I don't suppose I'll ever know. But I know it was this visit that resulted in the old brown photograph that formerly hung in the reading room of the Historical Association. I say "formerly" because one day Charles remarked, "Well, Edward, there aren't many eccentrics left these days, so I suppose we should encourage the few we still have;" and he made me a present of the photograph. It hangs above my desk as I write. Thanks to Susan's diary, I know much more about it now than I did when I first saw it.

For instance, I know now that Robert is a cadet in

the Colonel Andrew Belcher Stump Military Academy; and that he is scowling in order to keep from laughing, because a schoolmate of his (an older boy whom he worships, here on a weekend visit) is making faces at him from behind the photographer.

I know now that the bundle of blanket and lace that Mrs. Shaw looks down upon so tenderly contains John Thomas Shaw, Jr., who is fifty-one days old. (I also know that both Susan and Victoria were disappointed when he was named. Susan—perhaps with tongue in cheek—wanted him to be called George Bernard. Victoria was set on Robin Adair Beauregard.)

I once described Mr. Shaw's smile in this picture as "happy but faintly bewildered." I thought the faint bewilderment might be there because he was still having trouble believing what had happened. But there could be a simpler reason. One of the items in Susan's last entry is, "Daddy's repeater still missing." You can get a lot of bewilderment out of something like that. As for the happiness—who wouldn't be happy married to someone as beautiful as Isabelle? And who wouldn't be happy with investments in two young but thriving inventions, the telephone and the electric lamp?

I previously thought that Victoria had that faraway musing look because of general romantic tendencies. I was only partly right. The main reason for her expression in the photograph happens to be Robert's aforementioned schoolmate. He is tall, and comes from Virginia, and has courtly manners (when he is not standing behind a photographer) and his name is Talbot.

As for why Susan smiles—well, we know why. There is nothing more to add. But I must confess something. That smile, delightful as it is, irks me a little at times. It's so—smug; as though everything were *her* doing.

Sometimes I long to be able to say to her, "Susan, my dear, *I* had a hand in bringing about your happy conclusion, you know. And although you may think that your fortune is unique, I suspect that perhaps it isn't. Because I have a note from an old acquaintance of yours; a note written in a spidery hand on thick creamy paper. It begins, 'Reservations for this year are filled.' Do you see the implication, Susan? *For this year . . .*"

But I suppose it's just envy that makes me want to tell her that. She smiles because one year she was chosen. Whereas *I* can only hope. I keep telling myself that there are grounds for hope. The writer of that note knows me. This year, perhaps, or next year, or sometime—